Sharpe Shooter: Skeleton in the Closet

Cozy Suburbs Mysteries, Volume 1

Lisa B. Thomas

Published by Lisa B. Thomas, 2017.

SHARPE SHOOTER: SKELETON IN THE CLOSET

Prologue

Rookie deputies in the county sheriff's department always did the grunt work, especially when the boss was running for re-election and his opposition was throwing around accusations of mismanagement. It was June, just six months until the November election. Deputy Trey Simms ached to get out in the field where the action was instead of being stuck cleaning out the ancient back closets of the original Bingham County evidence room. How was he supposed to impress the boss doing clerical work? Most of the cold case evidence had long since been transferred to a warehouse in Maycroft, but this 3rd floor office was converted to a file room back in the seventies, and no one had bothered to empty out its three closets—until now.

So far, the most unusual item he had uncovered was a bowling ball cut in half and drilled out to hold a small Colt pistol. It came from a 1971 case where a woman took her dead husband's old Brunswick to the pawn shop. The clerk found the gun after dropping the ball, causing the pistol to fire. Luckily, no one was hit.

Like all the other items he had inventoried, Simms entered the case number and description into the master computer spreadsheet, marking it for transfer. He put the case file and broken ball back in the cardboard box and re-sealed it with new evidence tape.

Reaching for a yellowed cardboard box from the top of the metal shelf, he discovered this one was larger and heavier than the others. As he tipped it forward to get a hand underneath, dust fell like snow and landed on his hair and face. Setting it on the table of his makeshift workstation, he pulled out his dingy handkerchief to wipe off the debris, first from his face and then off the paper label on top of the box. It read, "Jane Doe 3-18-64." The cellophane evidence tape had long since lost its ability to secure the contents of the file box and fell away as he gave it a slight tug. Removing the lid, he peered inside at a black plastic container with a lid that was taped shut. Simms, however, recognized immediately what he had uncovered. Stunned, he shook his head. "Well, I'll be darned."

LIKE MOST TEXAS SHERIFFS, Bob Lowry was hands-on when it came to unusual cases in his jurisdiction. You aren't re-elected to office four times by trusting your deputies to do all the work. If a case proved important enough to make the newspapers, Lowry insisted his name appear in the article. He learned that playing nicely with the Maycroft Police Department worked to his advantage, and the two agencies were careful to keep off each other's toes. He ruled over the county like a protective father who could not trust his children to fend for themselves.

Deputy Simms understood this about his boss, which is why he headed straight down to the second floor with his Jane Doe evidence box in tow.

"What in the heck is this?" the sheriff demanded, wiping away dust that settled on his heavy oak desk from the filthy box.

"Take a look inside." Simms carefully removed the lid.

Sheriff Lowry stood up to get a better view. "Why on earth is there a skeleton in my evidence room?" he shouted as his face reddened. "Whose case is this? How long has it been here?"

Satisfied he had gotten the boss's attention, Simms answered calmly. "Sir, it's a Jane Doe from 1964, so it's been here roughly fifty years. Do you want me to find the original officer's name?" He opened the case folder for the first time and scanned the summary notes inside the cover, stopping on something unexpected.

"No! Take it over to forensics." Lowry pushed the box toward his newest deputy. "And Simms," he added. "As of right now, this is your case. And whatever happens, I want that skeleton in the ground as soon as possible. This could look really bad for me, so don't screw it up!"

"Yes sir." Simms quickly put the folder inside the box and replaced the lid. He hurried out of the office holding the box in front of him like an undetonated bomb. Around the corner in the hallway, he stopped and leaned back against the wall.

Not only had he unearthed some family's loved one, he had blown the lid on one of his own family secrets. Whether it was fate or coincidence, he knew it was up to him to solve this icy cold case.

Chapter 1

Getting canned after more than thirty years of teaching was definitely not on Deena Sharpe's bucket list. But there she was, packing up the last remnants of her classroom and the only career she had ever known.

The *tap-tap-tap* sound coming down the hallway meant Janice Marshall, the assistant principal, was ready for Deena to vacate the building. No one liked the screeching of finger-nails on a chalkboard, but most teachers at Maycroft High School would have chosen *that* sound any day over the incessant clatter of those clicking shoes. Like Deena always said, there was something fishy about a woman who could stand on her feet all day in high heels. She was not to be trusted.

Luckily, Deena would never again have to endure Janice Marshall's condescension or her shoes.

"How much longer are you going to be, Mrs. Sharpe?" Janice stood in the doorway as though entering the room might infect her with cooties.

"There's no telling. I might need a few more hours," Deena said, using her gooiest Southern drawl. "You don't have to wait for me, dear. Why don't you just run along and see if you can find some other teacher to harass."

Janice smirked and leaned against the door frame as if she herself were the very foundation of the building and began occupying herself on her cell phone.

Standing over her desk, Deena slowed her movements even more. "Is this how you deal with all teachers when they leave this school? Are you worried I might steal this stapler?" She held it up as a visual aid.

Janice rolled her eyes. "No, but this is a *special* circumstance."

Still holding the heavy black stapler, Deena contemplated bashing Janice in the head or shoving it up somewhere else. She envisioned the headline in the *Northeast Texas Tribune*: Ex-Journalism Teacher Bludgeons Assistant Principal with Swing Master II.

She dropped the stapler in the box she was filling to take home. *Ha!* Not exactly the gold watch others got upon retirement, but it would have to do.

Deena envisioned herself as Lara Croft: Tomb Raider—always ready to fight the good fight. In her mind, she would kick butt and take names; in reality, she would step aside and apologize. Still, she was always looking for ways to unleash her inner Lara. She even took karate at one time but gave up when she got smacked around by a six-year-old warrior princess.

"You know," Janice said, "this all started because you refused to cooperate with Principal Haskett. If you had just given his daughter that four-page spread in the yearbook like he asked, you'd still have a job."

"Four pages!" Deena shook her head and slammed the desk drawer closed. "No single student even gets two pages. The yearbook is not his personal scrapbook. Fair is fair."

Deena had considered just quitting when he made the unreasonable demand but mustered the strength to stand her ground. After several more meetings, Principal Haskett "suggested" that perhaps Deena's talents could be more useful elsewhere. He said she could stay until the end of the school year and officially resign rather than be fired but only if she kept the information under wraps until school was out.

Deena agreed, although she didn't give a hoot about whether people knew she was canned. Everyone in the small town of Maycroft knew all their neighbors' business anyway. So, she included the pages and turned in her resignation.

"Whatever," Janice said with a heavy eye roll. "Besides, you're probably super burned out after *all* those years of teaching. I'm surprised you lasted this long."

The heat rose from Deena's chest, up her neck, and landed in her cheeks. "Just how old do you think I am, Ms. Marshall?"

"You don't really want me to answer that, do you?"

Standing there in her power suit and heels, Janice Marshall was the complete opposite of Deena. Whereas Deena loved her teaching job, Janice was all business. She had taught health for the obligatory three years before becoming eligible for a job in administration. The students had liked her well enough, especially the boys. With her long brown locks and brooding dark eyes, she was one of those women who had perfected the hair-flip to her advantage early on in life.

Deena, on the other hand, had always wanted to be a journalist. But it just wasn't in the cards. She had been guided toward teaching by a college counselor and found herself in a high school classroom in the blink of an eye. She couldn't believe that was more than thirty years ago.

Deena balled her fists and put them on her hips. "Go ahead. Take your best guess."

"Judging by the dye job and those gray roots, I'd say sixty-five. Maybe seventy. Definitely old enough for social security and the senior discount at the movie theater."

Well, that didn't go like I thought. Deena raised her chin. "I'm fifty-nine, Miss Congeniality. And you have a *lot* to learn if you want to be successful in the education business."

"Yeah, right. Check back with me in six or seven years when I'm a superintendent."

That was all she could take. Deena had lost all the fight she'd been able to muster for Janice Marshall. Now, surrendering her classroom keys to the principal's chief stooge seemed like waving a white flag on her career. However, she still managed a pained, melancholy smile as she headed out of room 106 and down the hallway for the final time.

Was this the end? Was she destined to spend the rest of her life in a rocking chair shooing the neighborhood kids off her front lawn?

At that moment, Deena had no idea that one phone call would soon set her on an entirely different path.

Chapter 2

The Perry County Forensics Department consisted of two technicians and an intelligence analyst. Far from the sophisticated set-ups in big city police departments, the forensics lab mainly took fingerprints, gathered DNA samples, and bagged evidence to send to larger forensics contractors to be processed. Automobile accidents, burglaries, and the occasional cattle rustling kept the small team busy.

Trey Simms was not surprised when the lab tech told him it would be several weeks before she could even look at his fifty-year-old skeleton. He hoped calling it a "high priority" for Sheriff Lowry would speed up the process, but she only scoffed and said, "Everything is a high priority for Sheriff Lowry."

So, it came as a shock when less than a week later he got a message to call the lab about his skeleton from the closet.

"Are you aware that your vic was shot twice in the back of the head?" the tech asked.

Simms was very much aware, having spent several nights poring over the case files. The facts of the case were simple: A local farmer found the body in a low-lying area of his back forty in the southern part of the county. It was March, and the ground had begun to thaw. The victim was in his late twenties, according to the report. Due to the damp conditions, the body had badly decomposed and had been dragged—probably by coyotes—before it was found.

The deputy recovered two bullet casings from a Model 10 Smith & Wesson along with the skeletal remains. The victim had no identification and no personal belongings. The only recognizable scrap of clothing was a tattered piece from what appeared to be a green raincoat. The color of the coat led the deputy to believe it was a woman's garment. The report concluded that based on the size of the skeleton and the type of clothing found, the body was that of a female. The cause of death was gunshot wounds to the head, and the case was labeled a homicide.

With a lack of sophisticated scientific technology in 1964, common sense proved to be as big a part of crime solving as DNA evidence was today.

The report documented that over the next few months, numerous people were brought in to try to make an identification of Jane Doe. No one claimed the body, which was left inside the cold case closet to rot, along with the identities of the victim and the killer.

"There's not a lot left to work with here, Trey," the tech said. "I doubt computer recognition software could even help. However, I think the forensic artist we used on the Sorenson case may be able to sculpt a face from the skull."

"Well, that's good news, right?" The rookie was apprehensive, yet hopeful. Not only was the sheriff breathing down his neck on this case, he had a personal interest as well.

The tech sounded skeptical. "That work costs big bucks, and we don't have a family paying for it this time. Do you think the boss will sign off on it?"

"I'll talk to him and let you know."

"By the way Simms, you might also want to let him know this: Your Jane Doe is actually a John Doe."

Chapter 3

Deena flipped the pages of the latest issue of *Texas Monthly*. Tossing the magazine on the coffee table, she walked to the window to look out on the backyard for the hundredth time that day. The flower beds, once brimming with brightly colored blooms, were barren except for the occasional leafy weed standing defiant against the sun's crucifying rays.

Is this what it would be like from now on? As a teacher, Deena was used to having summers off. Those long, hot days were filled with attending workshops, reorganizing her classroom, taking a few short trips with her husband, and getting her house back in order before the next school year began. She also used the time to work on her vintage booth at the Hidden Treasures Antique Mall, a hobby she had turned in to a small side business. This summer was going to be different, and she had no idea what to do with herself.

Ah. Life in the suburbs. The sound of cars driving past the house, garage doors opening and closing, and children screaming for no real reason all signaled the end of the workday. It was only her third day to be at home, but already her house felt like a white-collar prison.

Deep cleaning her house was out of the question. With no children due to some wiring problems in her lady parts, she and Gary kept their ranch-style home tidy enough for their liking. Cooking was never one of her specialties. As a child, she'd preferred reading a book to helping her mother in the kitchen. What on earth was she going to do with her new-found freedom?

The sound of Gary's car pulling in was like a trumpet announcing the king's arrival. She glanced quickly in the mirror above the entry table, noting that Janice was right. It was time to color the gray roots peeking out from her auburn hair. Earlier, she had spent half an hour playing with her make-up as a way to pass the time. She looked like someone the make-up artist at the funeral home had just practiced on.

"I'm so glad you're home," she said when Gary walked in the side door from the garage. "How was your day?" She couldn't believe how June Cleaver-ish she sounded.

"Same old same old. It's weird having you here when I get home." Gary placed his briefcase and keys on the entry table and turned to look at her. "What did you do to your face?"

"It's called make-up," she said with a sneer.

"Did you use a mirror?"

"Very funny." She stood on tiptoes to kiss him and left a bright red smudge on his cheek.

She'd met Gary the first year she taught school in an East Texas town even smaller than Maycroft. He was a financial adviser and came to the school to discuss retirement plans for teachers. At just twenty-three years old, retirement was the last thing on Deena's mind back then. She sat in the auditorium, however, thinking how nice it would be to spend a little one-on-one time discussing her long-term future with the dashing Gary Sharpe. After the meeting, she got his business card and he got her phone number. They married a year later and moved to Maycroft for Gary's job ten years after that.

Looking around in mock surprise, Gary asked, "What? No dinner on the table?"

Deena shot him a look. "Just because I'm unemployed doesn't mean I've suddenly turned into Betty Crocker. If you wanted someone to cook and clean for you, you should have married your mother."

Gary loosened his tie. "You realize that's against the law, right?"

"I hope that's not the only reason you chose me over her."

The playful banter continued until Gary offered to take her out to dinner as long as she would clean off her face.

They drove to Las Abuela's, their favorite Mexican food restaurant. It was small and dark and served great margaritas and comfort food. There were plenty of other good restaurants in Maycroft, most filled with tourists or screaming babies. Except for the strolling mariachis on Saturday nights, the place was quiet and cozy. Maycroft thrived on tourism, mostly from the antique stores, flea markets, and bed-and-breakfasts. The locals, however, had their favorite haunts off the main street.

Gary took a sip of his drink. "So how does it feel to be retired?"

"*Unemployed*, not retired," Deena shot back. "For Pete's sake, there are plenty of jobs I can do."

"I know, but you don't have to work if you don't want to. Besides, you know how burned out you were. This is the perfect time to take a break and re-group. We can manage financially." He covered her hand with his. "I just want you to be happy."

There was that phrase again. Janice had called her burned out too. Still, the strong tequila and spicy salsa was lifting her spirits. "Hey, maybe I can come work for you. I could be your secretary or Girl Friday."

Sangria spewed out of Gary's mouth, covering the table-cloth with little red spatters. Once he wiped his mouth and regained his composure, he looked at her sheepishly. "You're kidding, right?"

She folded her arms on the table. "I was, but I guess I know how you'd feel about it."

"Sorry, but you took me by surprise. I love you more than anything, but being together all day, every day..."

"I get it." The server appeared with their food. She waited until the girl left. "But seriously, I was thinking about trying to get a job at the newspaper."

"Is that something you want to do? I didn't realize you planned to keep working."

"I think so, it's just..." She felt the old insecurities creeping up and looked down at the table.

"Just what?"

"You know what they say, 'Those who can, do. Those who can't, teach.'" She made air quotes to emphasize her point. "Maybe I can't."

Gary leaned forward, looking her straight in the eyes. "Deena Jo, you are one of the smartest people I know. You can do anything you set your mind to. Besides," he added, "the only reason you didn't become a reporter in the first place was so that you could be close to home to take care of your brother."

Russell. Deena's older brother was the family eccentric. Intelligent and creative, he served in the army and had returned home not quite the same. One of the reasons she decided to stay in Texas was to be near him. She had hoped he would marry, but it seemed he was destined to bachelorhood. That didn't stop Deena from setting him up on blind dates, though.

"Actually, I talked to Russell today," Deena said. "Have you heard his latest scheme?"

"What's he up to now? Building a spaceship or searching for Bigfoot?"

"He and some of his survivalist buddies are going to build one of those underground shelters for the next D-Day or the zombie apocalypse. They're like little boys playing army in the dirt."

They both laughed and shook their heads at the thought of Russell's antics, an endless source of amusement.

Gary raised his glass. "Well, here's wishing you much luck for the start of your new career, whatever it is."

She clinked her glass against his. "Move over Woodward and Bernstein. Make way for Sharpe."

Chapter 4

Before even one single lump of clay could be laid across the plastic model of the skull of John Doe 1964, Dr. Erin Sparks knew she had to add precise markers to key areas of the skeleton. Forensic anthropology relied on specific measurements to recreate the features lost by death and decay. It was a painstaking process, requiring an objective mind and an artistic eye.

She replaced missing parts of bone with plastic pieces carefully shaped to patch up the skull's tapestry, once perfect but now tattered and threadbare. The bullets had destroyed much of the back of the skull. The jawbones had to be secured. One eye socket was merely a splintered void. Like a mason putting up drywall, she knew all the seams would be perfectly hidden once she applied the finishing compound.

Like a buzzard circling its prey, Dr. Sparks walked around and around the mounted skull trying to determine if her calculations were correct and if each marker was in its proper position. Once the transformation began, there would be no turning back. She and her assistant had spent four days getting to this point. Satisfied at last, she was ready to begin the wet work.

Opening a fresh package, her fingers dug into the moist brown clay. She pressed it into the forehead section and smoothed it out as if performing a delicate facial massage. Every line, every crease had to be perfect. The work, slow and painstaking, would continue for several days.

Her lab assistant knew this was when Dr. Sparks herself transformed from scientist to artist. With the precision of a surgeon and the creativity of a sculptor, she began to reveal the face that time and the elements had stripped away.

Staring at the man who entered her life a stranger just a week earlier, Dr. Sparks contemplated his life and death. What had he done to be murdered in such a way? Was he an evil monster or an innocent victim? Where was his family? Had they lost hope after one, two, twenty years of waiting? Would anyone remember and identify him?

These questions kept her keen on getting the details just right. The mouth, quieted by an assassin's merciless act; the eyes, blinded by piercing hot steel—these were the most important features to capture, the critical keys to expression. Getting them wrong could be the difference between lying eternally in a pauper's grave or coming home with a hero's welcome. Day after day, she performed her magical resurrection.

Finally, on the afternoon of the last day, she stepped back and smiled as though meeting the man for the first time. She greeted him warmly. "Hello, John Doe. Nice to meet you."

AFTER THREE WEEKS OF waiting for Dr. Sparks to finish the model, Deputy Simms was ready to release the face of John

Doe 1964 to the media. Sheriff Lowry had said in an interview that the department owed it to the citizens of Bingham County to allocate the funds for a complete facial reconstruction sculpture to be made of the victim, especially considering how his predecessors had botched the original case. When the current forensics lab reassembled the skeleton, it was obvious the victim was male, not female.

The department had a lot riding on this case. Not only would they have to hope the artist's sculpture was accurate, they would also need people who had known the victim to recognize him and call in a tip. Fifty years of life can wipe away a lot of memories.

"Any of the tips worth following up on?" Sheriff Lowry asked at the end of the first day.

"Not so far," Simms said. "Mostly they have been crackpots claiming the vic was Buddy Holly or Jimmy Hoffa. I ran down a few names, but they were people who were never missing in the first place. The article ran in the Dallas paper yesterday and the Tribune today. Tomorrow it will be in the Ft. Worth newspaper and on some of the news stations. Maybe we'll get more viable tips."

"Let me know as soon as something useful turns up. We spent a piss-load of the county's money on this case, and I want something to show for it." Lowry picked up a file on his desk, a signal that meant Simms was dismissed.

Relief washed over him as he headed to the front desk to retrieve the stack of new messages from Renee, the receptionist. Luckily, the sheriff had not asked for any of the specifics that Simms would just as soon keep hidden.

"Anything good?" he asked.

"Only if you are still looking for Elvis." As the main receptionist, Renee was the first line of communications for the office. She had gotten the job right out of high school and could be counted on to screen the important calls from the quacks.

Simms scoffed and headed down the long hallway to his office. Sitting down at his desk, he picked up the John Doe flier off a stack of files. John Doe, he wondered, who are you?

The next morning the tips started pouring in. Most of the callers were not sure if the person they were calling about had ever gone missing, but the resemblance was "uncanny." Or so they claimed. Simms continued running names through the missing person database with no luck. Then Renee called asking him to come to the front desk.

"Whatcha got?" He stared at the large stack of messages in front of her.

She put two callers on hold and slid the notes toward him. "Look at this top message. This is the third caller who identified the same person. The other two are in the stack somewhere. Thought you might want to know." She pressed one of the blinking red buttons on the console in front of her. "Bingham County Sheriff's Office. Can I help you?"

Simms took the messages and headed back to his office. Matthew Meade, he read off the top message, are you our John Doe? Flipping through the notes, he found the two others that named the same man. Turning to his computer, he entered the name. Nothing. No hits. Still, this was his first real lead. He dialed the phone number on the first message.

"Fred Tucker? This is Deputy Trey Simms of the Bingham County Sheriff's Office."

"Oh yes," said the gravelly voice on the other end of the line. "I guess you got my message about Matthew Meade."

"Yes sir. What makes you think the picture in the paper is him?"

"Well, I grew up in Bingham, you see, and the Meade family went to our church. Their boy Matthew was a few years behind me in school." He coughed a few times before he continued. "After he got back from the army, he moved up to Maycroft. I remember that something happened and he disappeared. Right out of thin air."

"When was that?"

"Well, let's see now. That would have been some time in the sixties. Early sixties. I was living in Austin then but remember hearing all about it. Such a shame—a fine young man."

"Is there anything else you can tell me? Do you remember the names of any of his family members?"

"No. That's all I can remember for now. I'll think on it some more and call you back if I come up with anything."

"I would be much obliged, sir. Thank you for calling." Trey hung up the phone and turned straight to his computer just as Renee walked in.

"I'm taking a short break. Got anything?"

"Maybe," Simms said without turning around from his screen. He began searching the internet for everyone named Matthew Meade from Texas.

Renee slipped out the door, leaving him to his work.

There were more people with that name than he had imagined, so he telephoned the next lead, hoping she might have more information.

"I am so glad you called, Officer Simms. I have been nearly sick to death ever since I saw that picture in the paper. I am positively sure that is Cora and Frank's boy from Bingham."

Simms wrote down the names as he listened to the elderly woman's dramatic tale.

"Back in the early 1960s, '63 perhaps, poor Matthew disappeared off the face of God's good earth. He had taken a job up there in Maycroft instead of staying with his kin and going to work with his daddy at the market. That was bad enough. But then to disappear like that? All they found was his car. Why, Cora and Frank were beside themselves with worry. Wouldn't you be?"

"Of course."

"They hired a private detective and did everything they could think of, but they never did find that boy. You can imagine what people back home were thinking. No evidence of a crime. Just taking off and leaving his mama and daddy to worry themselves to death." She took a deep breath. "Now, I read in the paper that his dead body was found in a pasture just a few miles away in Bingham County and not long after he disappeared. And they thought he was a woman? Well, I'm just sick, I am."

"Mrs. Davidson, do you know how I can get in touch with the Meade family?"

"God rest his soul, Frank has passed. Cora is living with her sister in Ft. Worth, though. Let me just find my address book and see if I have their number." She set down the receiver.

Simms could hardly believe what he was hearing. His heart pounded and his hands shook a little as he waited for her to return. Deputy of the Year, he thought, picturing a gold plaque with his name engraved in bold letters. Lowry will shake my hand, and I'll get my picture in the newspaper.

"I don't have their telephone number, but I have their address. Do you have a pen?"

Simms wrote down the information and promised to call back. Just then, Renee stepped back into the office.

"Trey, there's someone on line three I think you want to talk to."

Glancing at the flier again, he picked up the phone and pushed the button to answer. "Deputy Simms here. Can I help you?"

"Hello. My name is Cora Meade. My son is Matthew Meade."

Chapter 5

Like a teenager applying for her first job at the movie theatre, Deena stood in her closet trying to find the perfect outfit to wear for her meeting with the editor of the *Northeast Texas Tribune*. She wanted to look like a "mature, responsible journalist" and not a "matronly, burned-out school teacher," even though that's apparently what she was. She had never cared that much about fashion and was regretting it as she searched her closet.

By this time in her life, Deena had grown comfortable with her appearance, except for those darn gray roots. She looked around her closet and suddenly hated all her clothes. Everything seemed too young or too old or too boring or too something. A whole new wardrobe was what she needed. Maybe she should cancel the appointment with Lloyd Pryor and go shopping.

Chicken, she chided herself. *You can do this.*

Finally, she decided on an old stand-by: a navy-blue pants suit and crisp white shirt. Okay, so it wasn't exactly crisp, but it would do. She added several pieces of turquoise jewelry. Heels would make her look younger, but flats would be safer, knowing she could be a little clumsy at times. She spotted a pair of red pumps she'd bought some years back to go with a dress she had only worn once. They would add a youthful flair without the worry of turning an ankle. She had gone easy on the make-up this time. Looking in the mirror, she declared her appearance "good enough," and headed out the door.

AN OLD BRICK WAREHOUSE from the seventies, formerly used to store used restaurant equipment, stood as the home of the *Northeast Texas Tribune,* a regional newspaper that served all the surrounding counties. It was the go-to paper to find out who died, who tied the knot, and who got caught with their hand in the cookie jar, business-wise, that is. Although they were not hiring, Deena knew the editor, and he had agreed to talk to her.

Once inside the building, she walked past several jeans-wearing, t-shirt-clad twenty-somethings, all glued to one electronic device or another. As she waited outside of the editor's office, her red pumps stared up at her like Dorothy's ruby slippers, and she immediately began re-thinking her choice of apparel. It looked like she was trying too hard. She tugged on her pants legs trying to cover as much of her shoes as possible.

Glancing through the office window, she saw Lloyd Pryor, editor-in-chief, talking on the phone. He was wearing a short sleeve shirt without a tie and a pair of khakis. She could just make out what appeared to be a coffee stain on his shirt. Feeling self-conscious, she pulled off her bangle bracelets and slipped them into her purse.

"Come on in, Deena," Pryor said and motioned to a chair.

She walked in quickly and took a seat, hoping he wouldn't notice her feet.

"So, you want to work for the newspaper." He sat down behind his desk, picked up a half-eaten sandwich, sniffed it, and tossed it in the trash.

"Yes sir. I thought I might try getting off the sidelines and into the game." She smiled, hoping to impress him with her enthusiasm.

The weary editor leaned back in his chair and swiveled, glancing down at his desk and then out the wall of windows at his newsroom. "There are easier ways to make a living, you know."

"I know. But newspapers are the lifeblood of a democracy and seeking truth is a noble occupation." The words had flowed out of her mouth without thinking, obviously part of a lecture she had given her beginning journalism students. "Besides, it seems like fun."

"Fun? Do these guys look like they're having fun?"

She followed his gaze out into the large desk-filled space and watched as reporters typed, talked on the phone, read each other's notes, and occasionally laughed as they tossed wads of paper in overflowing cans.

"You bet it does," she said.

His lips curled as he eyed her with amusement. "You know we can't pay you anywhere close to what you made teaching."

"Money is not an issue," she said and immediately regretted it. "I mean, it matters of course, but the main thing is that I want to write. I don't expect to get rich." She could only imagine what Gary would think of an applicant who said such a thing.

"Noble." He let out a sigh. "As I told you on the phone, the only opening I have now is in ad sales, and I doubt that's what you're looking for."

"No, you're right. The last thing I sold was Girl Scout cookies, and I ended up eating most of them myself."

"The gal who writes obituaries is going on maternity leave in a month or so, but that would be a waste of your experience."

"Ugh, who wants to write about dead people anyway." Deena couldn't believe she'd said that out loud.

"You'd be surprised," Pryor said, "the obituaries are the most read articles in any newspaper. People also love a good scandal or murder mystery."

She began to relax. "If I come across one, I'll let you know."

"I'm not suggesting you manufacture a story or anything, but if you hear of one of your neighbors bilking the PTA or housing a fugitive, you know who to call. The summer is the slowest time of year for juicy news. People are too hot to go outside and water their yards much less commit crimes."

Deena laughed. "Got it. Although, you aren't suggesting you wish the good citizens of Maycroft were less law abiding, are you?"

"Of course not," he said more seriously. "I live here too. I have kids. But human nature has a way of balancing the good with the bad. We just want to be able to report on it."

"Fair and balanced. I get it."

"How about this," Pryor said, and sat upright. "You spend some time writing for one of the online sites to brush up on your skills and show me what you've got. Check back with me in about a month, and I'll see what I can do. Things get busier around here in the fall."

Deena crinkled her nose. "Online sites? You mean like blogging?"

"No, definitely not blogging. Here's a list of three pretty good ones. They're looking for all kinds of articles, mostly informational, for publication online. You could even earn a little money in the process. It's a type of freelancing. You'll understand once you look into it." He jotted down the names and passed her the paper.

"That sounds great." She was lying, of course, and shook his hand. "Thanks Lloyd. I appreciate your taking the time to talk to me."

"Don't be discouraged," he said. "A great story might be just around the corner."

She forced a smile and nodded. As she turned to head out the office door, she could feel her spirits sinking. Also, she felt sure he was staring at her stupid red shoes.

Chapter 6

Deena sat at her computer, busily typing out the meaningless article that would probably never see the light of day. Her mind wandered. Maybe she could take up a new hobby. There was knitting, yoga, or maybe she could read to the blind. Did the blind still need to be read to? With all the great audiobooks out there, they could probably get almost anything they needed on their own. She jotted herself a note to look up "reading to the blind" for a potential new article.

Her cellphone rang, giving her a chance for a much needed brain break. Even talking to a telemarketer would be more interesting than writing this dribble. *Yes, I most certainly* do *want to hear about your new health care plans.*

She answered the phone expectantly. "Hello."

"We found Matthew," the voice on the other end of the line said.

"What?" Deena's heart skipped a beat. She had not talked to her aunt, Lucy Lancaster, since Easter. Her voice was raspy but recognizable.

"We found my brother, Matthew," Lucy repeated more slowly. "It turns out his remains were found in an old creek bed near here back in March of 1964, about five months after he disappeared."

A gasped slipped out of Deena's mouth as she counted the years. "That was more than fifty years ago! Why did they never contact Gran and Grandpa?"

"You'll never believe this. Not in a million years." Lucy always had a flair for the dramatics. "Back then they identified him as a woman, so they never connected it to Matthew. That's why Mama and Papa were never called in to try to make an identification of his remains."

"A woman?" Deena had vague memories of her Uncle Matthew, mostly from photographs she had seen. "I know he was tall and thin, but a woman?"

"I know it sounds crazy, but that's what the detective said."

Deena shook her head. "Where has his body been all this time?"

"A few months ago, they found his skeleton in an old storage closet at the sheriff's department and used the skull to form his face. They put a picture in all the local newspapers."

"That was Matthew? I saw that picture in the *Tribune*, but never made the connection."

"That's right," Lucy said. "Luckily, someone Mama used to go to church with thought it looked like Matthew. She called us, and Mama called the Sheriff's office. A deputy came up here to Fort Worth and got pictures of Matthew and a DNA sample from Mama. Yesterday they called us and, sure as I'm sitting here, it was a match!"

"Well I'll be." Deena could hardly believe what she was hearing. After nearly fifty years, the Great Meade Family Mystery was finally solved. Her long-lost uncle had been found.

Even though Matthew had long ago been declared dead, she knew her grandmother had always held out hope that he'd be found alive.

Lucy continued. "We are going to have services for him on Saturday in Bingham so he can lay to rest with Papa. I can tell you more about it then. I don't suppose your mother will fly back here from Hawaii, but will you call her?"

"Of course." Deena walked into the den and wrote the information on a memo pad. "So how did Gran take the news?"

"Not very well. She has been in bed for the past two days."

"Poor thing." Deena promised to be there on Saturday and thanked Lucy for calling. "One more thing," Deena said before hanging up. "Do they know how Uncle Matthew died?"

"Bless his heart. He was murdered!"

Chapter 7

Russell Sinclair was three years older than his sister, Deena. He was high spirited and well liked. He rarely talked about the time he spent in the army, at least not to Deena, but it was obvious that the experience changed him.

After he was discharged, he tried to get on with his life, despite the bouts of PTSD. He went to college, but had a hard time concentrating. Eventually, he found work with a buddy from high school who owned an appliance repair shop.

Deena was afraid the stress of the news about their Uncle Matthew would trigger one of her brother's migraines, so she was relieved to see his car pull up to the house right on time the day of the funeral.

"You look nice," Deena said. "I was afraid you'd be wearing shorts."

"I pulled out my 'good' jeans just for this occasion." Russell rarely wore anything other than cargo shorts, a Hawaiian shirt, and flip flops. People said he looked like Jimmy Buffett.

Deena insisted Russell sit in the front seat so he and Gary could talk baseball and politics on the drive to Bingham.

Russell turned toward Deena. "By the way, sis, how did your interview at the newspaper go?"

"It wasn't really an interview. They don't have any openings now. He said I should submit articles to online sites to brush up on my writing skills."

"Hmm. Anything I should read?"

"Oh sure," she said sarcastically. "Fascinating stuff. If you want to know the twenty most popular fireworks shows or how to host a backyard barbeque for vegetarians, just let me know."

Russell snickered. It wasn't long until the front seat conversation turned to sports.

Deena stared out the window, lost in her memories. When she was growing up, she had loved visits to Gran's house. She recalled the faint odor of mothballs mixed with the strong scent of Estee Lauder. Green wallpaper with sweet pink roses covered the walls of the bedrooms, even Matthew's.

His room was not kept as a shrine, per se, but rather a place where he could walk in any moment and return to the way things were when he went off to join the army. It was always freshly dusted with the bed made and the curtains opened. From what Deena could tell, Gran kept secret treasures in an old cedar chest in the corner of the room. There seemed to be an unspoken rule that no one was to open that chest. As far as Deena knew, it stayed that way even when her grandmother moved in with Aunt Lucy and Uncle Frank.

Upon the urging of her children, Gran finally had her son declared legally dead four years after he disappeared so she could redeem his insurance policy and stop being bothered by their incessant letters. In Gran's mind, that was just paperwork, something to satisfy the hunger of the IRS.

As the years crept by, Gran began giving away some of her prized possessions: her carnival glass punch bowl set, her porcelain figurines, and even her brightly colored Fiestaware dishes. However, she never gave away any of Matthew's belongings.

"You're doing it again," Gary said, interrupting Deena's train of thought. He looked at her in the rear-view mirror.

"Doing what?"

"Staring out at the road looking for you-know-what."

"Actually, I wasn't this time," she protested.

Russell turned in his seat. "Looking for what?"

Gary chuckled. "Didn't you know your sister searches the highway for dead bodies?"

Russell glanced at her over his shoulder. "What, like dogs and armadillos?"

"No, people." Gary shot a grin back at Deena.

"And they call *me* the nut job in this family." Russell shook his head in wonder.

"It's not like that," Deena said. "I think I do it subconsciously most of the time. It's because of Matthew. I hear stories on the news about two drunk fishing buddies hanging out by the lake and, 'lo and behold,' they come across a dead body. I want that to be me—the finder, that is, not the body."

"Why on earth would you want to stumble across a corpse?" Russell asked.

"I guess after watching Gran worry and wonder all those years with no answers, I just want to be the one who could bring news and maybe closure to some suffering family."

"You should have been a detective," Russell said. "Remember how you used to spy on me as a kid and then rat me out to Mom and Dad?"

"Only to keep you from getting into more trouble."

"Hey," Russell said, "maybe you could write about Matthew's case. Seems like it would make an interesting story. You could include all the behind-the-scenes stuff."

"Maybe." That had been one of the first things Deena had thought of when her aunt had uttered the word "murder." But would others think she was exploiting a family tragedy? Maybe not. "I guess it wouldn't hurt to poke around a little. See what I can dig up."

Gary shot her a look in the rearview mirror. "Not the best choice of words."

"Oops." She leaned back in her seat. Before she realized it, she was staring out the window, searching the sides of the road for anything suspicious.

THE GRAVESIDE SERVICE was awkward at best. Her aunt, uncle, cousin, and a few neighbors showed up out of respect. Frank Meade, Matthew's father, had died of a heart attack about eight years after his son's disappearance, proving it was indeed possible to die from a broken heart. Matthew's mother, Cora, was the strong one who never gave up hope she would one day find her missing boy. That's why Deena was worried when it turned out Cora, her grandmother, was too upset to attend the funeral.

Aunt Lucy had said she would give more information about Matthew to Deena at the services, but she couldn't. There were no more details to give. Everything her aunt knew matched the article Deena had read in Tuesday's Dallas newspaper.

Deena covered Aunt Lucy's hand with hers as they waited for the service to begin. "You know my heart just aches to think of Gran having to wait and worry all those years when Uncle Matthew's body had been found just five months after he went missing. We should sue them or something."

Lucy nodded and her headful of curls bounced in the sunlight. She had faithfully colored her dark blonde locks despite the passing years. They suited her. She had creamy skin and blue eyes like her mother. "I know, dear. It just doesn't seem fair. And learning he had been killed like that? Shot in the head? No wonder Mama couldn't find the strength to come."

"If they'd realized Matthew was a man, maybe they could have found out who killed him, at least. And Gran and Grandpa wouldn't have wondered all that time if their son had just abandoned them."

"That's true," Lucy said. "You know there were all kinds of ugly rumors about him, like him being a gangster in the mob. Some people even thought he might be in a cult. Dreadful rumors. I know he was my brother, but he was a little odd."

Deena leaned away. "I can't believe you'd speak ill of the dead. Let's hope lightning doesn't strike you down." She looked around at the gravesite. There was no casket, only a raised area under the green Astroturf that draped the headstones of other members of the Meade family. Her cousin Mark had driven up to the Bingham County Sheriff's Office to retrieve the remains. Apparently, they fit in box the size of an old Samsonite suitcase.

Uncle Richard, Lucy's husband, began the service with a series of prayers. Then he invited others to share memories they had of Matthew. There was a long, awkward silence as people fanned themselves and lowered their eyes as if lost in quiet reflection. Finally, Russell broke the tension by telling a funny story about Uncle Matthew taking him to the circus as a young boy. Whether a tall tale or not, everyone laughed and shook their heads in appreciation. A few others offered their own stories.

These vague recollections shed little light on the man they were memorializing fifty years after his death. It was as if they were burying a ghost who had no real form or presence. No one cried, but all took solace in knowing the family was together now in a "better place." Deena made a point to talk to Gary about where they planned to be buried when their time came. Funerals tended to do that to people.

Outdoors late June in Texas was no place for the living or the dead. It was the kind of heat that literally left your skin feeling seared, like a piece of raw meat on a sizzling griddle. No one lingered around the cemetery for small talk. Friends and family got on the road, back to their safe existences where people did not disappear without a trace and did not get shot to death.

Deena, on the other hand, found herself drawn to the gravesite of the uncle she had barely known. She had watched Gran suffer too long to just erase him from her mind.

After everyone else left, she stood under the awning, sweat running down her face in place of traditional tears, and said a private prayer. As she walked to the car to join Gary and Russell, she had a sneaking suspicion the life and death of Matthew Meade would haunt her.

She just never imagined, however, it would be so soon.

Chapter 8

Something about the urgency in Aunt Lucy's voice sent a cold chill through Deena. The calm demeanor Deena had witnessed just three weeks earlier at Uncle Matthew's funeral was gone. A feeling of dread gripped Deena by the throat. "What's the matter? Is it Gran?"

"She's not dead, if that's what you're asking. But emotionally, she's a wreck. I was wondering if you might come for a visit. Richard and I need to talk to you about something."

"Of course," Deena said without hesitation. "I can drive over in the morning."

After ending the call, Deena wondered what her aunt wanted to talk to her about. Had they been thinking about death too? It couldn't be about their will. Their son, Mark, would be getting their inheritance. She'd have to be patient and wait until she got there.

But Deena wasn't a patient person.

The next day she hit the road early. Never had she seen so many 18-wheelers on one stretch of highway. The drive west was always more backed up than the eastbound lanes. Her mind wandered as she slowed down, stuck behind one huge truck after another. She could smell the lemon pound cake she had bought at the supermarket, unpackaged, and then re-wrapped in foil to make it look homemade. Her mother had taught her never to show up empty handed when you go a'calling.

Deena's mother had always warned her that Lucy was the drama queen of the family. Matthew had been the stable one; Deena's mother Margie was the dreamer. After Matthew disappeared, the two sisters had drifted apart.

Glad to be away from her computer, Deena thought about the latest tedious, boring article she was slaving over for *Post-It-Here Pages*, one of the online writing sites that Lloyd Pryor had suggested. So far she had written twelve articles on topics ranging from "Top 10 Places to Visit in East Texas" to "How to Keep Rabbits Out of Your Garden." Her latest article was entitled, "Twenty-five Facts About Labor Day."

Nobody gives a rat's ass about Labor Day, Deena thought when researching information for the article. Only reason anyone cared about it was that they got a day off from work. Still, she had pressed on, hoping one of her stories might strike a chord with Lloyd Pryor.

She passed several antique shops and had to force herself to keep driving. Besides having her own antique booth, she collected pottery and porcelain figurines. Vintage junk was like heroin, and she was definitely an addict.

After more than an hour on the road, Deena finally parked her blue Explorer in front of Aunt Lucy's house. As always, pink roses trailed along the fence despite the hot Texas sun. It was a wonder anything could survive around there.

Lucy opened the front door and welcomed Deena inside. "Come on in," she said and gave Deena a hug. "Mama is sleeping, so we'll be a little bit quiet."

They walked past the living room straight to the large country kitchen with its round oak table and bay window. A pitcher of sweet tea and a plate of sandwiches were set out on the kitchen table. Richard set aside the newspaper and stood up to welcome Deena. Lucy thanked her profusely for coming up to see them as she unwrapped the pound cake and put it on a plate. After a bit of small talk, Lucy became more serious and folded her hands on the table. She reminded Deena of a character straight out of *Gone with the Wind*.

Was she about to say a blessing? Deena swallowed down a bite of chicken salad sandwich she hadn't waited to bite into.

"Deena," Lucy said slowly, "we asked you here for a favor. Several years ago, I made a promise to Mama. She knew her health was failing and was worried she was going to die. She asked me to look after Matthew if he ever came back home." Tears began to well in her eyes, and she reached in the pocket of her housedress and pulled out a handkerchief. "Although I knew that would never happen, I told her I would."

Deena reached over and patted her aunt's arm.

"A few days ago, Mama woke up in the night all in a terror. She said she had seen Matthew's ghost in her room, rummaging through the cedar chest. She thought it was a sign that he was not able to rest in peace and needed help." Lucy wiped back more tears and blew her nose loudly.

Deena narrowed her eyes. "A ghost? Bless her heart. I'm sure it was just a bad dream. Nothing to worry about."

"I know, but now she's been asking me to try to find an explanation for my brother's death. She doesn't think he'll rest until then. I don't know what to do." She put the back of her hand to her forehead and swooned dramatically. "I don't want any dead spirit lurking around my house."

Richard sat with his head down and his arms folded across his chest. Was he as worried about Gran as Lucy? Deena wasn't sure.

"I understand," Deena said. "Have you thought about hiring a private detective?"

"We have," Richard said, looking up at last, "but something happened last week that kind of spooked us. There was a man that came by here asking us all kinds of questions about Matthew. He said he was an investigator, but he didn't seem like any investigator I ever knew. I asked him what he was investigating, and he said, 'the murder of Matthew Meade.' We assumed he was a police detective helping to find Matthew's killer."

Lucy picked up the story excitedly. "He seemed to know all sorts of things about Matthew and Mama and Papa." Then she whispered, as though an intruder waited in the next room. "He wanted to know about Matthew's old friends and people he worked with. He had some pictures of Matthew when he was in the army. He even asked us about people with foreign-sounding names."

"Not just foreign," Richard added. "Russian."

Oh great. Were they worried about the cold war now? Deena braced herself for whatever was coming next.

Richard walked over and took something off the kitchen counter. "I asked this fella which police department he worked for. The man hemmed and hawed then pulled out this card." Richard handed Deena the simple white business card.

She set down her half-eaten sandwich to read it aloud. "Leon Galt, Investigative Journalist, New York City, and a phone number. Not much information." She looked up to see their worried faces.

Richard peered at her over his reading glasses. "That's when I told him that we just as soon not answer any more of his questions, and he left. It was all suspicious." He looked at Lucy who had lost some of the color in her face since they'd begun talking.

"Does Gran know about this?" Deena asked.

Lucy picked up he cloth napkin and began to fan herself. "No, luckily she was asleep in the back room when he was here."

Deena thought about the mysterious visitor. "Did you ask him why he wanted this information?"

Richard glanced across the kitchen toward the front room. "I did, but it was like he just ignored the question and kept talking. I can't believe we told him as much as we did."

"Maybe you should call the police." Deena wasn't sure what else to suggest.

"We did," Richard said. "They said to let them know if he ever shows up again. They had never heard of him before and couldn't do anything since he hadn't broken any laws."

Deena, still holding the business card, just sighed. "I really doubt you said anything that would cause any harm. Sounds like maybe he's writing an article of some sort. Maybe he really does want to help find out who killed Matthew." Deena hoped her positive tone would lessen the anxiety that clearly gripped her aunt and uncle. "Did you say anything to Mark about this?"

"Oh yes," Lucy said. "Our boy was the one who suggested we call you."

Deena hesitated. "I'm glad you called, of course, but why me? What is it you want me to do?"

Lucy glanced at Richard. "You have always been so clever, dear," she said. "Everyone says so. You won all those writing awards in college. Since you are retired and know all about this reporting stuff, we were hoping you would look in to this Galt fellow and into Matthew's death for us and for Gran."

"Okay, but what exactly do you want me to find out?"

"We want to know who killed Matthew and why," Richard said bluntly.

Deena glanced back and forth between the two. Were they serious? She couldn't hide her look of disbelief. "You realize you are asking me to solve a fifty-year-old crime. I really doubt I can do that—I doubt anyone can do that." Not even Lois Lane.

"We understand," Richard said. "But if there is something important enough for this man from New York City to come all the way down here to Texas to find out, we want to know what it is. You may not find all the answers, but at least you could figure out what he wants."

Lucy folded her hands as though she were about to start begging. "We could hire a stranger to investigate, but like Mark said, you never know who to trust. You are family, so we know we can trust you. We'd do it ourselves, but at our age..."

"I understand," Deena said. "But why didn't you ask Mark? He's retired, right?"

"He volunteered, but we said no." Richard sat back and folded his arms. "Let's just say that Mark has a way of mucking stuff up. Just ask his two ex-wives. He's not really good on the follow-through, if you know what I mean."

Deena stood up and walked to the window that looked out over the backyard. The more she thought about it, the more intrigued she became. This was just the kind of meaty story that could get Lloyd Pryor's attention. Anything was better than writing about Labor Day. This could be her chance to do some real reporting and show people what she was made of. She turned back around. "I can't make any promises, but I will see what I can find out."

Relief washed over their faces, and Lucy threw her arms around Deena. "Thank you, dear. This means a lot to us. I know Mama will be happy to know someone is actually doing something to bring closure."

Richard walked over to the far side of the room. "Mark came by yesterday and helped me pull some boxes out of the attic. These are Matthew's papers and such that Gran had collected." Richard tried to scoot the cardboard boxes across the floor using his foot. At almost eighty years old, his back wasn't what it used to be. "Maybe there's something in there that can help. Also, keep a list of your expenses. We'll cover all your costs."

Deena nodded and stared at the boxes. What on earth had she gotten herself into? She took the business card and stuffed it in her pocket. A plan was already starting to hatch. First things first. Who was Leon Galt and what was he doing stalking her family?

Chapter 9

By the time she walked through the garage door to the house, Deena knew exactly what she wanted to do first. She went straight to the den and sat down at the large oak desk she had bought at an auction. She had painted it white to match the country cottage feel of the room. Many times since, she wished she had left it the original warm brown color with all its former bumps and bruises. The older she got, the more she appreciated things in their natural state.

The fatigue of the long drive melted away as she waited for her computer to wake up and get to work. She felt certain that an internet search for Leon Galt would spring forth a fountain of information. Rather than a fountain, though, she got a flood. Thousands of results came back for that name. She added quotation marks around it and watched the results narrow to a few hundred. Scrolling through the first few pages, she could not find anyone who fit the description. She tried adding search terms such as "New York" and "investigator" and "journalist," but she still came up empty. A dentist, a veterinarian, a plumbing service—she would have to dig deeper to find this guy.

"Hey," Gary said as he entered the room.

Deena jumped and caught her breath. "Geez, you scared me. I didn't hear you come in. Good thing I didn't go all mad dog on you."

"Why are you working in the dark?" He flipped on the overhead light that Deena had been too anxious to bother with.

"You are not going to believe this," Deena said as she watched her husband settle into the cushy chair next to the front window.

"Aunt Lucy and Uncle Richard want me to investigate Matthew's murder. Actually, they want me to *solve* it, but we all know the chances of that happening are slim to none. They gave me some boxes of Gran's things, which I need you to get out of the car for me. And get this—they are covering my expenses."

"Deena Sharpe, P.I." Gary laughed and crossed his legs.

Actually, Deena really liked the way that sounded. She pictured herself with binoculars and a walkie-talkie peering out from behind the bushes at some seedy motel. "I agreed to do it because I think it will give me real investigative experience and make for a compelling story to show Pryor."

"You know, that's not a bad idea. Besides, your relatives are really getting up there in age. I'd hate to think this is hanging around their necks." He walked over and sat down on the corner of Deena's desk. "But if you take on this project, who, my dear, is going to tell the world twenty-five facts about Labor Day?"

Deena grimaced and smacked her husband on the leg. "Very funny. Now will you please go get those boxes?"

She got up and cleared a space in the middle of the floor. Sitting on the throw rug, she could sort through all the contents, hopefully finding clues. She felt like a doctor performing exploratory surgery, looking for anything that seemed suspicious.

"What do you want to do about dinner?" Gary asked when he returned, his arms taut with the first heavy load.

"I'd like to start going through these boxes right away. Could we just get pizza delivered?"

"Pizza it is," he said, taking off his tie and heading to the bedroom. Deena followed him to get comfortable, knowing she would be sitting on the floor for a long while. She pulled on a pair of plaid flannel pajama bottoms and a t-shirt.

"Want to look through the boxes with me?" she asked.

"Not unless you need me. The Rangers are on tonight, and I need to proofread a report I have to send out tomorrow."

Deena anticipated that he would decline her offer. Just like when they were first married and she would ask him to help her grade papers, he would always have something else more pressing. It established an expectation that she took care of her teacher work and he did his financial business. Obviously, nothing had changed. And that was fine with her.

Deena practically salivated with expectation as she removed the lid of the first box, not knowing what secrets might lay within. The odor of dust and musty old paper filled her nose and made her throat tickle. She felt like an archaeologist when first unveiling a hidden treasure. The inside of the box was jumbled and stacked full. She decided to separate the contents into piles of similar items.

Photographs, mostly black and white, comprised the top layer of the box. She stared at the people in the pictures, her eyes squinted, mind intent, mood hopeful. So many of the faces seemed familiar—were probably relatives—but were unidentifiable to Deena. She placed the photographs into two piles: with Matthew and without Matthew. She came across a few snapshots of her mother and father, lingering on these longer, drifting back in time. These particular pictures tugged at her heart, making her more melancholy than usual.

The doorbell rang, and Gary went to pay for the pizza. Brian, one of her students from the past school year, stuck his head around the door to say hello.

"Hi Brian. I see you're back delivering pizza again this summer?"

"Yes ma'am. Last time, though, since I graduate next year." He hesitated then added, "Mrs. Sharpe, is it true you quit?"

"Yes. I'm going to miss you guys, but I was just ready to graduate from high school myself. I wanted to try doing something different."

"Yeah, I get that. Well, see you around." Gary closed the door behind Brian and then insisted Deena stop what she was doing to eat.

"So, what's in the boxes?" Gary asked before chomping down on a slice of pepperoni.

"From what I can tell by just glancing, there are pictures, old bills, letters, postcards—just a little bit of everything." She filled two glasses with wine and sat down on the counter stool. "I don't really know what I'm looking for. Hopefully, I'll recognize something important if I see it."

"Be sure to pay attention if you see a letter from Matthew that says, 'If I am found dead, here's who did it and why.'"

"More jokes, really?"

"You know I'm just playing. I want to be supportive, but this seems like a wild goose chase."

"I know." Deena wiped the corner of her mouth and took a sip of wine. "I've been wondering, though. What are the main reasons a person would kill someone else?"

"Well, let's see. Anger...revenge...money...greed."

"Also, jealousy or to keep him quiet. I'm sure there's more reasons, but that's a good start. So, what might be in those boxes that could tie Matthew to one of those reasons?"

Gary nodded. "I see where you are going with this. If you find something showing he owed someone a lot of money, you might have a motive."

"Right. Or a love letter from a girl who turns out to be married. You know, this is going to take a lot more digging than I thought."

"Unless, that is, you find that letter I mentioned."

"Ha," Deena scoffed. "By the way, is that lipstick on your collar?"

"What? Where?" Gary anxiously tried to look down at his shirt.

"Gotcha!" Deena ate and thought about her next move. "I'm going to call the Bingham County Sheriff's Office and make an appointment to meet with that deputy who worked this case. Maybe there is some additional information that can help me retrace what happened when Matthew disappeared."

"Do you need me to go with you? I'd have to reschedule—"

"No," Deena interrupted. "I'm a big girl. I can do this myself." She ate a few more bites of pizza.

Something gnawed at her, trying to make its way from the back of her mind to the front. A sense of foreboding came over her. "By the way, have you ever heard of a man named Leon Galt?"

* * *

THE NEXT MORNING, DEENA got up to tackle the boxes again. After pouring a cup of coffee, she returned to the den and her ever-growing stacks. Most of the pictures of Matthew were portraits taken when he was young. She loved the ones of him in short pants and a bow tie.

After about an hour of looking through faded photos and greeting cards, Deena's legs ached from sitting on the floor. She got up and went to her desk to call the sheriff's office. A receptionist said she could meet with Deputy Simms the next morning.

Looking at the three boxes, she decided to change tactics since she was not making much progress. Pouring out the contents of all three boxes, she shuffled through the mounds of papers, looking for legal documents. Among the insurance policies and old report cards, she found papers related to Matthew's military service. He received an honorable discharge from the U.S. Army in 1954 at the rank of TEC III. She made a note to look up what that meant.

Several hours passed, and she still had not discovered even one piece of information that would bring her closer to learning about Matthew's death or the mysterious Leon Galt. Then she had an idea. In her address book, she found the phone number she was looking for. She dialed one of her former journalism students who was currently working for a publisher in New York City.

She was connected to Paula Reynolds and proceeded with the usual chitchat. After a few minutes, Deena explained her reason for calling. "Have you ever heard of Leon Galt?"

"The name sounds vaguely familiar, but I can't place it. Why? Who is he?"

"He claims to be an investigative journalist out of New York, but I haven't been able to find anything out about him. It's a long story, but I was hoping you might know who he is."

"The division I work for publishes mainly technical books and manuals, but I'll ask around and see if I come up with anything." Paula promised to call back within a few days, and they said their good-byes.

Deena considered calling Galt directly, but she wanted to get the scoop on him first. She looked back at the growing mess in the middle of the floor. The piles mocked her, or at least that's how it felt. Something, anything, she thought. And just like that, a clue found her. It was a photograph of Matthew with a pretty blond, and it appeared they were more than just friends.

Chapter 10

Deputy **Simms** had warned Deena over the phone that there was not much more information he could offer beyond what was written in the newspaper, but he would be glad to meet with her anyway. The news article was a follow-up story explaining the details of Matthew's identification, including quotes from Sheriff Lowry. It stated that the case remained an open investigation.

She arrived at the sheriff's office expecting the inside of the building to look like the police departments on television, complete with officers sitting out in the open at their cluttered desks, ringing rotary dial telephones, and surly perps in being led away in handcuffs. She was disappointed to walk in and see just a counter with a receptionist. The place could have passed for a dentist office.

After signing in, she was escorted down a long hallway to Deputy Simms's office. She had expected to be frisked or at least scanned with a hand-held metal detector, but no such luck. She waited in the doorway while Simms finished his phone call, observing that the inside of his office looked a lot like Jake's, the loan officer at her bank. The small metal desk was tidy, the file cabinets were lined up in neat rows, and nothing screamed "Criminals Beware!" She took solace, though, when she saw a half-eaten donut on the side of his desk. Not a total let down.

Simms hung up the phone and walked around his desk to greet her. He offered coffee and water, which she declined. She noted that the attractive young deputy had good manners. He must have come from good stock.

"Mrs. Sharpe, I have your uncle's file right here." He opened the inch-thick manila folder. "We located the missing person report and have the original notes on the investigation. We have now combined that with the file on the recovery and identification of the body."

"Are you the one who found the skeleton in the closet?"

Trey nodded. "Yes, ma'am. But it was Sheriff Lowry who made the decision to try to make an identification."

He obviously knew where his bread was buttered. Deena pulled a legal pad out of her black satchel and flipped it over to a fresh page. "Any information you can give me would be helpful." She clicked her pen and sat poised ready to take notes like a 1960s stenographer, wishing she knew shorthand.

"Besides the information that was in the newspaper, we have the name of the restaurant where Mr. Meade ate with friends on the evening he disappeared: 4 October 1963."

This was just the kind of juicy nugget Deena was dying to chomp on. "Go on."

"He had dinner with two work colleagues, Gene, that's g-e-n-e Collins and Donna Morrison, usual spelling. They ate at the Park Street Café in Maycroft, which, as you probably know, is no longer there."

"Were Gene and Donna interviewed? Do you have any notes on what they said?" Deena anxiously clicked her pen.

"It just states that they ate dinner and then all left around six-thirty. Neither saw anything suspicious." Simms cleared his throat and kept his eyes on the file. "People from his work and a few neighbors were questioned, but no one had seen or heard anything out of the ordinary."

"Was there any other evidence taken?"

"Yes ma'am. The lab took some fingerprints from the car, but they all belonged to Matthew Meade. Two former army buddies who were living in the area at the time were also interviewed. Their names were not listed in the report."

Deena noticed the deputy's face flush. She wondered why he felt uncomfortable.

"There is a note, though, that both gentlemen commented they were surprised there were eyeglasses found in Mr. Meade's car."

"Is that because he couldn't see anything without his glasses?" Deena asked, anticipating his response.

"No, ma'am. They didn't think Mr. Meade wore glasses. They said he had been a sharpshooter in the army and had perfect vision."

Deena made a note and put a star next to it. "So, the day after he disappeared, his car was found with his keys in the ignition, his wallet on the seat, and his glasses on the dashboard. Was anything else found in the car?"

"That's it. Also, you probably know that his parents searched his apartment along with a deputy and found nothing suspicious."

Deena had not known that. She leaned back in her chair. "Matthew's mother, Gran, told me once about hiring a private detective."

"The file has no information about that. From what I can tell, there was no evidence of a crime, so the investigation was minimal. It was treated like a missing persons case. Seems like some people just thought he took off."

Deena scribbled some notes but knew they would be useless.

"There is one last thing I thought you might be interested in seeing." Simms walked over to the shelves that lined one side of the office and gently took down a small plastic container. He brought it over and set it on his desk. "This is the scrap of clothing found with your uncle's body." He looked at Deena before removing the lid. "Not everyone has the stomach for this kind of evidence."

Deena stood up and moved closer to the desk. Simms pulled out a plastic bag containing a large stained swatch of green cloth. She noted that the fabric at one time had been shiny, like the yellow rain slickers people used to wear. "That's it?" she asked. "Deputy Simms, I taught high school for twenty-nine years. I've seen worse than that on the floor of the girls' bathroom."

Her humor broke the tension, and Simms laughed as he returned the evidence to the shelf. "My wife is really squeamish, so I like to ask just in case."

"Thanks," she said and stepped back from the desk. "What I find the most disturbing about the case is that Matthew's body was identified as a female and not a male. And you say it was because he was wearing a green rain slicker? That one mistake cost our family years of heartache and let someone else get away with murder."

"Yes, ma'am. I understand. The deputy who investigated must have thought the coat belonged to a woman.."

Deena looked at the list of questions she had made prior to coming. "Do you have the name of the officer who conducted the original missing persons investigation?"

Simms shuffled through the papers in the folder. He appeared nervous again. Then without looking at the file, he said, "Deputy R.G. Brice." Deena wrote the name in her notes.

"I assume he no longer works here after all this time."

"No, he doesn't. He died."

"Oh...sorry."

"Here. I made you a copy of the ballistics report." He pulled the paper out of the folder and handed it across the desk. "I hope this information helps."

"Will you or anyone else in the department be working on the case to find out who killed Matthew?"

"As you probably know, ma'am, cold cases like this are not high priorities for the county. I'll follow up if any tips come in, but I seriously doubt they will." He closed the folder in front of him. "The person who committed this crime probably got in a lot of trouble in his life and spent most of it rotting away in prison. I'm just glad we were able to make the identification so your family could get a little closure."

"I'm sure you're right." She put away her notepad and pen.

"I understand you are looking in to this matter for Mrs. Meade. I got to visit with her when I went up there to get the DNA sample. Nice lady."

"She wants me to find out whatever I can. Also, I'm a...*writer*." The word sounded awkward to Deena as she said it aloud. "I am planning to write a story about the case when I get all the information I can."

Simms cocked his head. "That's a coincidence. A man called me a few days ago asking for information about the case. Said he was writing about it, too."

Deena's jaw dropped a bit. "By any chance was his name Leon Galt?"

"Yes, it was."

Chapter 11

About twenty miles southeast of Maycroft lay Crossbow, a small town of about eight hundred people living on large plots of land. Unlike Maycroft with its tourist spots, thriving businesses, and neat rows of homes in well-planned neighborhoods, Crossbow had the feel of the Old West, which is just how the residents liked it. They had few city ordinances other than burn bans when the summer drought was at its peak. People were free to hunt, shoot off firecrackers, and leave burned out cars and rundown barns just as they pleased.

Russell Sinclair liked living in Crossbow.

When his neighbor Cliff's wood-frame house burned down, Cliff decided to build his new brick home, complete with a target range and swimming pool, on the edge of his property line so he and Russell could be in closer proximity for backyard barbeques, particularly on Sundays when the Cowboys were playing.

On her drive back home, Deena decided to make a quick detour to her brother's house. His knowledge of guns and weapons might be helpful. When she parked the car, she heard Russell's yellow lab making sure everyone was aware of her arrival. When no one answered her knock on the front door, she followed the panting dog around the side of the house. Russell shouted from Cliff's yard, so she walked over to the gate.

As she got closer, she saw the two of them sitting on lawn chairs inside Cliff's empty swimming pool. "What in the Sam Hill are y'all doing?"

"We're just testing out our new bunker," Russell said and spread his arms out like Vanna White to showcase the set-up.

She looked down at the empty pool. They had transformed it into an underground man cave. Besides the lawn chairs and beer cooler, they had a small, archaic television atop a wobbly TV tray along with a large electric box fan. The television scratched out some unrecognizable sporting event.

"What on earth is this?" Deena asked, hands on hips, staring at her brother.

"Isn't it great?" Russell said. "As it turns out, most of this area is solid limestone, so we gave up trying to dig. Then Cliff had the brilliant idea for us to use this giant hole that he had already paid someone else to excavate."

Deena shook her head in disbelief.

"All we have to do is build the top, and we got us a man-made, underground, kick-ass bunker." He gave Cliff a fist bump and then motioned for another beer. "We're going to convert the pool equipment to work as a sewage pump, get all battery-operated appliances, and add shelves to the shallow end. The diving board is still a bone of contention."

"You could *never* get away with this in the suburbs. I can't imagine why you are still single," she said with sisterly affection. Deena looked back over her shoulder at Russell's house. "Can we go inside to talk? I'm melting out here."

"Sure thing." He unplugged the box fan, and they all headed back to the house.

Russell lived in a three-bedroom ranch built in the late sixties. They walked through the sliding glass door into the den with its knotty oak paneling and wood-burning fireplace. The well-worn gold sofa and matching club chair reminded Deena of her childhood home. Russell's prize possession, a brown leather recliner, sat to one side of the laminated coffee table. Deena folded and stacked the newspapers strewn across the sofa and sat down. Cliff sat in the club chair, knowing the unwritten rule about never sitting in another man's recliner. Russell set the fan on the old Magnavox stereo console that used to be their father's and headed to the kitchen to get his sister a bottle of water.

"Thanks," she said, opening it and taking several big swallows. She pulled papers out of her satchel and handed her brother the ballistics report she had gotten from Deputy Simms. "Ever seen one of these?"

Russell took the papers and sat down in his chair. "Let me get my cheaters." He leaned toward the coffee table and pushed around some hunting magazines until he found his reading glasses. "Sure. It's a ballistics report." After looking it over for a minute, he asked, "Is this about Uncle Matthew?"

"Yes. I'm planning to write a story about him. One of those unsolved mysteries that everybody loves to read."

"That sounds interesting," Russell said. "How'd you get this?"

"I drove up to Bingham and talked to the deputy who worked the case. He gave me some details I hadn't known as well as this report. Since you are the gun expert in the family, I thought you could explain what it says."

Cliff's eyes widened. "A real-life whodunit. If you need any help, let me know." Deena hadn't thought about recruiting a side-kick. However, she would indeed need someone at the other end of the walkie-talkie if she ended up doing serious sur-veillance.

"Well," Russell said, looking back and forth between the pages. "The bottom line is that Matthew was shot twice at close range with a Model 10 Smith & Wesson."

"Is that a handgun or a shotgun or what?"

Cliff chuckled and the two men exchanged amused glances.

"It's a handgun. Here, I'll show you." Russell stood up and headed into one of the spare bedrooms. Deena could hear him open the metal door of the gun safe.

"Tell me, how does a person grow up in Texas and not know anything about guns?" Cliff asked.

"How does a person live in Texas and have a swimming pool without water?" she shot back.

"She's got you there, Cliff," Russell said as he walked back in the room. "Now this here is a Colt, but it's very similar to the Model 10. Want to hold it?"

"Not really, but I guess I should for the sake of research. Is it loaded?"

"Of course not," he said. "Do you think someone as wacko as I am would be safe around a bunch of loaded guns? In fact, you won't find a single round of ammunition on this entire property."

She looked at her brother incredulously. "But you have so many firearms? What about protection? What if someone breaks in?"

"Don't you worry about that." He reached down and scratched the top of his dog's head. "I got Maggie here for protection, plus I keep a Louisville Slugger right next to my bed."

Deena just shook her head. Her brother was full of surprises. She took the gun, which was heavier than she had expected, and pointed it toward the door. "So back in the sixties, who would have used a gun like this?"

"Bad guys, good guys, cops—basically anyone with a holster and need for fire power." He took the weapon back from Deena and passed it over to Cliff who was obviously interested as well.

"Have you ever shot it?" Deena asked.

"Oh sure, at the gun range. It packs quite a punch."

"I see. So, knowing this is similar to the type of gun that killed Matthew, does it point to any particular type of shooter?"

"About all I could say is that it probably wasn't a woman. No offense or anything, but it is a pretty big gun to be handled by a girl."

"Good point." Deena drank the rest of her water and got up to take the empty bottle to the kitchen. Her cell phone rang.

It was Paula. "I just have a minute before I have to go into a meeting," she said. "But I wanted to tell you what I found out about Leon Galt."

"Great." Deena hurried back to the sofa to get her notepad.

"He's an author. He writes under the name of Noel Future. Most people know him just by his pseudonym."

"What sorts of things does he write?"

"Conspiracy theories. Non-fiction, if you can call it that. Apparently, though, he is well respected as a writer. Not as 'out there' as you might think. Look, I've got to let you go. Search for him on the internet, and you will see some of his articles and books."

Deena thanked her and hung up. "Wow," she said and finished writing her notes. "Have either of you ever heard of an author named Noel Future?"

They both gushed at once. "Yes, of course."

Russell's eyes lit up. "Are you kidding? He's amazing."

Surprised by their enthusiastic reaction, Deena looked back and forth between the two. Then she nodded her head knowingly at her eccentric brother and his best friend. "Oh yeah. Of course, you have."

Chapter 12

The following day was Saturday, and Deena could hardly wait to get to her hair appointment. These gray roots age me ten years, she thought. In an hour or so I will be a new woman.

The Manely Beauty Salon was less crowded than usual. "Where is everyone?" Deena asked as she sat down in Kristy's chair.

"Anyone in their right mind has gone to the coast or up north on vacation to get away from this heat." Kristy wrapped a plastic drape around Deena's neck. "Are we doing the usual?"

"Yes, but maybe go a little shorter. I need to look younger."

"Don't we all, honey," Kristy laughed. "I'll mix up your color and be right back."

Deena looked around at the other clients to see if she knew anyone. It was the polite thing to say "hi," even if you saw your worst enemy. A young mother was trying to get her toddler son to hold still so the stylist wouldn't cut off his ear. An older woman was getting her hair set with rollers as she probably had every Saturday morning for the past twenty years. Barbara Cummings from the elementary school was getting her hair cut but had her back to Deena. Another woman was at the hair wash station, so it was hard to tell who she was.

"Okay, here we go." Kristy stepped on the bar to raise the chair. Handing the bowl of dye to Deena to hold, she made a part in the center of Deena's scalp and then brushed on the color. The strong smell of the mixture made Deena's nose twitch.

"So, anything new with you?" Kristy asked without giving her client a chance to answer. "I heard about your uncle. Such a shame to find out all these years later that he was murdered. I still don't know how they couldn't figure out he was a man. We do have different parts down there, you know."

"Apparently his skeleton wasn't intact, and they didn't have the DNA tests we have now."

"Well, I can't even imagine how you must feel. It reminds me of one of those mystery stories you see on TV."

"Speaking of mysteries," said Cheryl, the stylist at the next station, "did you see that story on the news the other day about that rich man in Galveston?"

"No. What about it?" Kristy asked.

Deena was glad the conversation had turned to another topic. As Kristy and Cheryl chatted, she reviewed what she had learned about Leon Galt, a.k.a. Noel Future. He had four books: two on Roswell, one on the NASA moon landing, and one on the CIA. His name popped up in forums about Princess Diana's death, Watergate, John Lennon, Jimmy Hoffa, Elvis, 9/11, and JFK. Apparently, he never met a conspiracy theory he didn't love.

So why was he investigating Matthew? Was his death part of some evil plot to take over Texas?

She watched as Kristy methodically applied the color to her roots. She worked quickly, which is one of the reasons Deena liked going to her.

Deena decided her first priority was tracking down the two people Matthew had dinner with the night he disappeared. She had a plan. Like she told Gary, if you want to find out about somebody in a small town, there is only one place to go: spaghetti supper after Sunday service. She would also bring along the photo of Matthew with the mystery woman to see if anyone recognized her.

"I'm going to sit you over here while I cut this little girl's hair," Kristy said and led Deena to the other side of the shop. "Here are some magazines."

She chose a copy of *Southern Living* and began flipping through the pages. Looking up from an article about bluebonnets, she saw the woman who had previously been getting her hair washed. It was Janice Marshall. Knowing she was trapped, Deena looked over and smiled, nodding her head. Janice returned the gesture. Deena pretended to read the article.

I thought I was finished with her when I left the high school. At least she isn't wearing heels.

At that moment Deena became more determined than ever to get enough information about Matthew's death to write an article that would knock the socks off people like Janice Marshall. She would show them she could walk the walk *and* talk the talk. Sure she had been a journalism teacher, but that didn't mean should couldn't be a journalist herself. She got up, holding her head high and started to walk out of the shop.

"Deena!" Kristy called out. "Where are you going? I'm not finished with your hair."

Oops. She'd have to hold off on her gallant march to success just a little while longer.

Chapter 13

The largest building in Bingham was the courthouse, originally built in 1892. Entering the town from the east, it could be seen from miles away. The second largest building was the First Methodist Church. That is where the Meade family had attended services for at least three generations and where Deena was headed on Sunday morning. Walking through the large carved church doors, she knew today she was searching for something other than God.

About fifteen minutes remained before service would be over, so she slipped into one of the rear pews and sat next to a young woman anxiously rocking her baby and trying to keep a pacifier in his mouth. After the closing prayer, the minister welcomed visitors and new members, read announcements from the bulletin, and invited everyone to stay for the spaghetti lunch. All donations would benefit the youth ministry's trip to Six Flags, he said. After two rousing verses of "How Great Thou Art," the congregation began making its way out the door. A crowd headed to the Fellowship Hall. Deena waited a few minutes before getting up to leave, wanting time for the food to be set out and people to be seated.

As she entered the hall, she located the ladies room to kill a few more minutes. Feeling enough time had passed, she checked her appearance in the mirror. Not too much make-up, a simple floral dress, black flats—she knew she fit right in.

The line of hungry Methodists had formed quickly, and she spotted the usual fare of spaghetti, salad, and French bread. She headed to a round table covered with a white tablecloth at the end of the buffet line where several women were filling plastic cups with ice and sweet tea. She thanked them as she picked up a cup, put a dollar in the donation jar, and cased the room for a place to sit. She was looking for the 80-ish crowd, people who might have known Matthew when he lived here.

She spotted a group that seemed to fit the bill. They were sitting at a rectangular table covered with white butcher paper that served as a disposable tablecloth. She walked over and sat down. A few people looked up and smiled.

"Hi. I'm Deena Sharpe." No one seemed to hear. "My grandparents are Cora and Frank Meade."

"Oh, is that so," a woman with her hair in a snowy white bun said. "How is Cora? Is she still living with her daughter?"

"Yes. She's well, but she's just having an awful time coping with the news of her son Matthew's murder."

The gentleman sitting next to Deena, cutting his spaghetti with a knife and fork, belted out a few words with gruff authority. "Terrible. Tragic."

"So, you must be here to visit the cemetery. It really is the best place to find comfort," another woman said.

"Well, no. Actually, I am writing a story about Matthew's death and was hoping to find some people who knew him."

"She's doing *what*?" a woman farther down the table asked.

"She's writing a story," the gruff man yelled back.

"Oh," the woman replied flatly, and everyone turned their attention to another woman showing pictures of her new great-grandbaby. Deena knew she couldn't compete.

That didn't go very well. She excused herself, although no one heard, and made her way to a different table. This one was round and filled with all women except for one lone man.

"Mind if I sit here?" she asked.

"Not at all, dear," a kind woman with a pretty blue hat said. "I don't believe I have seen you here before. Are you new to town?"

"No, I'm just visiting from Maycroft." Deena spoke her words carefully. "Cora and Frank Meade are my grandparents. I am on my way to the cemetery to visit Frank's and Matthew's graves. It really is the best place to find comfort," she said and sniffled, trying to bring a few tears to her eyes. "Poor Uncle Matthew."

"Oh goodness, dear, everything will be fine. Ladies," she announced, "this is Frank and Cora granddaughter, and she stopped by on her way to the cemetery. She's just sick about the death of her poor Uncle Matthew."

Like the hallelujah chorus, the sweet women all began shaking their heads and speaking at once.

"Can I get you some more tea?"

"You need to eat, my dear. Dorothy, fix her a plate of food."

"They are putting out brownies for dessert. Let me just get you a couple. Chocolate makes everything better."

And just like that, she was in.

"I'm Harriet. How is Cora? Such a shame she wasn't able to make it to the funeral service. Have you found out any more about Matthew's death? He was a fine young man."

"Did you know him?" Deena asked politely and then took a bite of her salad.

"Why yes. I think we all did." The other women shook their heads. "Roger, did you know Matthew Meade?" She practically shouted the question across the table to the man who was apparently hard of hearing.

"He was older than me, but I knew him," Roger replied.

Deena reached for her handbag. "I have a picture of him. Would you all like to see it?"

They most definitely did. She retrieved the photograph of Matthew with the blonde woman and handed it to Harriet who admired the photo and turned it over to see if anything was written on the back.

"Who is this pretty girl with him? I don't remember her." She passed the picture, which slowly made its way around the table.

"I have no idea," Deena said. "Do any of you recognize her?"

Several of the women speculated, but all their guesses were ruled out. "That picture was taken after he got back from the army. Maybe that is someone he met when he moved up to Dallas," Harriet said.

Technically, Matthew had lived in Perry just northwest of Dallas, but many folks in Bingham referred to any place "up north" as Dallas. The picture made its way back to Deena. Laying it reverently on the table in front of her, she addressed the group. "There are two other people I have been wondering about." Her audience seemed anxious to help her out. "Does anyone remember a woman named Donna Morrison?"

They talked it over and unanimously agreed the name was unfamiliar.

"There were some Morrisons living over in Hamilton, but they had all boys," Roger offered up.

Deena put her hands in her lap and crossed her fingers under the table. "How about a man named Gene Collins?"

"Sure, we know Gene," Harriet said and got confirming nods from the group. "The Collins family have had people here for a long time."

"Didn't Gene go up to Dallas with Matthew and work for a time?" Dorothy asked.

"That's right," Roger said. "He moved back not long after Matthew went missing."

Thrilled by the news, Deena cautiously asked if he were "still around."

"He's actually in Restwood," Harriet said.

Uh-oh, she thought. That sounded like the name of a cemetery.

Seeing the concern on her face, Harriet quickly said, "Restwood Nursing Home is over off Pecan Street and Elm."

Deena breathed a sigh of relief. "I may go visit him, if y'all think that would be okay. He was one of the last people to see Matthew alive, and I..."

"We understand, dear," Harriet said, patting Deena on the arm. "I think that would be fine."

Deena thanked them for their kind hospitality and promised to come back again to visit. Walking out to her car, she felt a little guilty for manipulating her new friends but decided real reporters do what they have to in order to get a story. As she headed out of the parking lot toward Pecan Street, she failed to notice the black Ford sedan slowly following her.

She found a spot to park near the front door. Taking a deep breath, she looked out the window of the car at the aging building in front of her. It appeared to have once been a well-maintained, tan brick building intended to reflect a homey and welcoming atmosphere. Much like the residents within, the years had taken their toll and the building was showing its age.

Opening the glass door, the smell of ammonia mixed with pine trees, the kind of odor that gets in your sinuses and stays there for days, smacked her in the face. She walked up to the reception desk and signed her name on the spiral notebook for visitors. Next to her name, she wrote "Gene Collins" as the resident she was there to visit.

The receptionist chatted with a nurse. She finally turned to Deena and asked, "Can I help you?"

"I'm here to see Gene Collins."

"Nancy, is Mr. Collins still eating or is he done?"

"I'll go check," the young nurse said.

Deena waited, wondering if the receptionist would ask about her relationship to the resident or her purpose for the visit.

Nurse Nancy returned. "He's asleep. Probably won't be up for at least an hour. Do you want me to wake him?"

"No," Deena said. "I'll come back later."

"Suit yourself."

Disappointed, Deena walked out and got back in her car. She thought about going to the antique store around the corner but decided to drive over to the cemetery, keeping her promise to Harriet & Co. It was probably bad karma to lie to old women.

Chapter 14

Nurse Nancy escorted Deena to Gene Collins' room about an hour later. "You must be a lawyer," she said.

"No. Why would you think that?"

"Any time someone here gets two visitors in the same day, at least one of them is a lawyer."

They stopped in front of room 319, and Nancy knocked on the door before opening it. "Here's another visitor."

Deena walked in and Patti walked off. "Hello, Mr. Collins. My name is Deena Sharpe."

"What do *you* want?" he asked suspiciously. "Are you a reporter, too?"

"Me? No. I'm Matthew Meade's niece." She stood in the doorway hoping for an invitation to enter. The man inside looked older than she expected.

"I see. Excuse me then." He pushed himself about halfway up out of his chair, fell back down, and said, "Come on in and sit down."

The room was about the size of the old motel rooms where Deena's family used to stay when they took trips in their big station wagon. The space was furnished with a hospital-type bed and a round table with three chairs. A small bureau and nightstand were pushed next to the wall by the bed. A television sat on a rolling cart.

"Let me just turn off the TV." He picked up the remote with a shaky hand. "What can I do for you today Miss —?"

"Please, call me Deena."

"Deena. I suppose you want to ask me a lot of questions about Matthew just like the other fellow."

"I didn't realize you were going to have another visitor today or I would have come another time."

"Don't put off what you can do today because tomorrow you might be dead."

"That's true, I guess," Deena said awkwardly. "Was the other man named Leon Galt by any chance?"

"Leon. That's right. Said he was an investigator. I asked him who he was working for, and he said it was an independent investigation. I answered a few questions and he left."

"Well, I'm here because my grandmother, Matthew's mother, asked me to see what I could find out about Matthew's death."

The old man nodded. "And since I was with him that night, you thought I might know something. How did you find me, Miss Deena?"

"I talked to Roger and Harriet and Dorothy at church. They told me you were here."

Mr. Collins reached over, picked up a small plastic pitcher, and poured water into a paper cup. "Want some?"

Deena declined.

"You know, I must have thought about that night a thousand times, and I still can't figure out what happened. Matthew and I knew each other since we were kids. We enlisted together.

When he got out and found a job, he found me one, too. We were like brothers."

"Where were you working?" Deena started to reach for a notepad but thought better of it, not wanting to come on too strong.

"We worked at the Barnes Medical Supply Company in Maycroft. Matthew was a manager, and I worked in the warehouse. He was a smart one, he was." He stopped to take another drink of water. Deena noticed his hands, fingers bent, skin dark and dry.

"Can you tell me what happened that day—the day Matthew disappeared?"

"I gave my friend Donna a ride to work that day. She said her front fender was busted up and she needed a ride. After work, I told her that Matthew and I were going to the diner, just like we did every Wednesday, and did she want to go along. She said 'sure' because she needed a ride back home anyway. She said she would call her brother and ask him to pick her up from there. She rode with me, and we met up with Matthew at the Park Street Café."

An attendant appeared in the doorway and reminded Mr. Collins that he needed to take his afternoon pills. She picked them up from the nightstand and gave them to him. He swallowed them down with a few gulps of water and she left.

"Where was I? Oh yes, so we ate supper and had us a good talk. Didi gave us our tickets and Donna was watching for her brother. It had started raining hard. A real gully-washer. You could barely see out the big front window of the diner. I got up to go to the men's room and when I got back, Donna was gone. Matthew was standing up at the register with Donna's coat and check. He said she had run out so fast she had forgotten to pay. I said I would cover it, but he said no. He waited for me to pay, then we ran out to our cars and drove off." He looked down at his hands. "I never saw him again."

Deena reached in her purse and pulled out the photo of Matthew and the woman. "Is this Donna Morrison?"

He looked at the picture and whispered, "Kitty." He appeared to lose himself in time for just a moment. "No. That's Kitty, uh, Katherine. I can't think of her last name. She and Matthew were sweet on each other for a while, but he ended it." He handed the photo back to Deena.

"Do you know why?"

"Once he told me that he didn't feel comfortable getting too close to people. He was a loner and seemed determined to stay that way."

Deena looked down at the smiling couple in the picture. She slipped the photo back into her purse. "When did they discover he was missing?"

"The next day, he didn't show up for work. That was unusual, but we figured he was sick or something. When he didn't come in on Friday, they called his apartment and he didn't answer. They called me out of the warehouse to ask me if I knew where he was. I said no. That's when they sent the police over to check. Nothing. They called his parents, but they had no clue where he was. A few hours later, the police found his abandoned car over on County Road. You probably know what happened from there."

Deena did. Everything Gene was saying seemed to make sense. She thought about the questions written on her notepad.

"Do you remember if Matthew wore eyeglasses at that time? They said they found his glasses in the car."

"Yeah, he wore glasses. Big horn-rimmed ones. Did you know he was a sharpshooter in the army?"

"I did not," Deena fudged. "What exactly did he do in the army?"

"He did a lot of...um, special assignments. Top secret stuff. Wet work."

"Wet work?"

"Sniper work. He never talked about it, of course. He swore an oath of secrecy. He must have been good, though, because he made TEC III real fast. That kind of stuff can mess a guy up."

"Do you think it messed Matthew up?"

"Maybe. I don't know." Gene looked across the room at the television, and Deena sensed he was getting tired of talking.

"Did you keep in touch with Donna Morrison?"

"No. She left town about a week after night at the diner. I heard she moved up to Oklahoma to be near her folks. It seemed like odd timing since Matthew had just gone missing."

Deena stared for a moment at a crack running along the side wall revealing layers of green paint under the latest beige color. She pictured a small interrogation room with a single-bulb light dangling over the table, she on one side, the suspect on the other. Time to get serious. She leaned forward and asked, "Mr. Collins, is there anything else you can tell me about Matthew's disappearance? Something you may have left out when you talked to the police?"

Collins, unintimidated by her show of strength, leaned back in his chair. "It's funny, you know, how people say he disappeared, like he was a ghost or a lady in a magic act. He didn't disappear. He was ambushed, probably kicking and fighting, and then they shot him." His eyes moistened and his voice cracked. "He didn't deserve that. No one deserves that."

The room seemed to grow darker. It was getting late. "Who do *you* think killed Matthew?" Deena asked.

"I hate to say this, but I think Matthew was mixed up in something. Something bad. And they killed him because of it. And it's not just me who thinks that, so does that reporter. And he says he can prove it."

Chapter 15

"**All human beings** are commingled out of good and evil." Deena mulled over this quote from Robert Louis Stevenson as she drove back home. As much as she hated to admit it, she knew it was true.

How could Gene Collins think Matthew was involved in some wrongdoing? Her childhood memories of him were of a sweet, kind man. She was determined to do right by Matthew no matter what he had done.

By the time she pulled into the garage, it was dark. All her thoughts were riding a mental rollercoaster. Relief washed over her when she walked in to find Gary pouring wine and preparing hamburgers on the backyard grill. The smoky smell of mesquite chips, comforting and familiar, drifted through the house.

"You always seem to know just what I need," she said and gave him a lingering hug.

"Do want to eat in here or outside?"

"Outside. I could use some fresh air."

They carried their plates and drinks out to the table beneath the covered patio. Gary lit the citronella candle in the middle of the glass-top table.

Taking a few sips of wine, Deena sat back, enjoying the cool breeze coming from the overhead fan. She watched her husband take a bite of his burger, knowing he was letting her relax before asking a lot of questions. She wondered how there could be any evil commingling in this wonderful man. Maybe Stevenson was wrong.

"I talked to Gene Collins," she said at last and took a bite of creamy potato salad. "He is in a nursing home in Maycroft."

Gary looked surprised. "I'm impressed. How did you find him?"

Deena told him about the church ladies and the cemetery and the nursing home. She also told him about Leon Galt's poorly timed visit.

Gary's face showed a hint of concern. "It seems a little coincidental that he would have gotten there right after you first tried to visit. Do you think he was following you?"

The thought had not occurred to Deena, but it seemed possible and caused her stomach to quiver. "How would he even know who I am, much less know where I was?"

Gary nodded. "You're probably right. What do you plan to do next?"

"I'd say it is time to give Mr. Leon Galt a call and find out what he's up to."

"I don't want you meeting with him alone."

Gary's quick response alarmed her for a moment, but she knew he was just being protective. "I won't. I promise."

Gary set down his glass and cleared his throat as though a speech were coming on. Deena was well aware of the signs.

"Look," he began, "if you want to drop this whole murder thing, I would totally understand. Lucy and Richard will get over it. And Gran, she may not even know what's going on. At her age—"

"Stop. I know you're worried about me, but I'll be fine. Just because Leon Galt writes crazy conspiracy theories doesn't mean he's dangerous."

Gary sighed and picked up his glass.

"You know," she said, "I have always believed that things tend to work themselves out. I'll never understand tragedies like Matthew's, but I think following through might be the best way to find a sense of justice."

Gary nodded. "You know I will support you in whatever you do."

Once again, Gary managed to make everything all right. They stood up and gathered their dishes to take back into the house.

Leaning across the table, she blew out the candle and set her sights on confronting Leon Galt.

Chapter 16

The screeching of the garbage truck brakes startled Deena out of a sound sleep. She was surprised she had slept past nine o'clock until she remembered the wine from the night before. She sat on the side of the bed to get her bearings. The phone rang, and she debated whether to answer it or let the machine pick it up. "You get it," she said aloud in the direction of the nightstand. Probably just a sales call.

The distressed sound of her brother's voice stopped her, and she raced over to grab the receiver. "Russell?"

"Oh, hey sis. I was wondering if you could do me a favor?"

"Are you okay?"

"I've got a doozy of a headache and just took my last pill. Could you run by the pharmacy and pick up my refill?"

"Of course. I'll leave here in just a few minutes. You just rest now."

She got ready quickly, pulling her shoulder-length brown hair back in a ponytail. It was rare for her brother to ask for help these days, so she knew he must feel awful. She poured herself a glass of orange juice and set about pulling food from the refrigerator to take him. Luckily, Gary had grilled two extra hamburger patties. She put the foil pack in a plastic grocery sack along with the leftover tub of potato salad. She grabbed a couple of cans of Dr. Pepper and her purse before heading out the door.

At the pharmacy, she bought a half-gallon of milk and a box of Raisin Bran, Russell's favorite cereal. She made the twenty-minute drive to his house in fifteen minutes. Holding the bags of food, she could hear Maggie barking and scratching on the other side of the door. She fumbled with her keys, trying to find the right one. She opened the door, and Maggie jumped up, almost tripping her as she tried to get to the kitchen.

"Here girl." She slid open the patio door to let out the grateful dog. Walking into the bedroom, she found Russell groggy and lying fully clothed on top of the covers.

"Hey sis," he said without opening his eyes. "Sorry to make you come all the way out here."

"No problem. How are you feeling?"

"Like road kill. This one hit me fast."

She looked at the nightstand to see an empty prescription bottle and glass of water. "Is it time for another pill yet? It's about ten-thirty."

"Not for another hour."

"Let's get you more comfortable," she said, pulling off his sandals. His floral Hawaiian shirt was soaked with sweat. She unbuttoned it and got a fresh t-shirt from the dresser. "Can you put this on?" Still lying with his eyes closed, he went through the motions of removing his other shirt and pulling the t-shirt over his head. She pulled the sheet up over his legs and turned on the ceiling fan. Like a child, helpless and needy, he let his sister care for him. This was all too familiar for them both. "Have you eaten?"

"No."

"I'd feel better if you would eat something."

"I'd feel better if you *didn't* make me eat something."

His snarky remark was a good sign, and Deena relaxed a bit. "Where's Cliff?"

Russell lay still as if trying to think. "San Antonio to see his son's family. Back tonight."

Cliff and Russell watched out for each other. Deena and Gary drew a lot of comfort knowing Cliff was right next door in case anything happened. "We're morgue buddies," Russell would say. "We check on each other once a day in case one of us has died and we need to call the morgue." The thought was bittersweet. Cliff had lost his wife to cancer two years earlier.

She walked back to the kitchen to put the food away. The milk carton in the refrigerator was almost empty and a few days past its expiration date. She threw it in the trash and tied up the bag to take out when she left. Maggie's bowls were both empty. She opened the cupboard and scooped out two big portions of food and let her in from the backyard.

Maggie trotted into the bedroom to check on Russell. Apparently satisfied that he was all right, she came back, went straight to her bowl, and lapped up the fresh water. Deena turned on the box fan and sat on the sofa. She decided to wait until it was time for Russell's next pill before she left. Maggie returned from the kitchen, tail wagging, mouth dripping with water. The large dog sat on the floor next to Deena, resting her head on Deena's knee. "You sweet baby." She reached down with both hands to scratch Maggie's neck.

She thought about her conversations with her friend Sandra who often encouraged her to adopt a shelter pet. Deena always gave the same excuse: She did not want a dog to have to stay home alone all day while she and Gary worked long hours. He loved dogs and would have several if she would agree. Secretly, she never wanted to admit, even to herself, that the reason she worked late at school so often was that she did not want to come home to an empty house—empty of children, that is.

Her cell phone and she dug it out of her purse. "Hello."

"Mrs. Sharpe, this is Leon Galt."

How had he gotten her number? "Yes, this is she."

"I understand you are looking into the death of your uncle, Matthew Meade."

"That's right." Her response was tentative.

"I spoke to Lucy and Richard Lancaster, and I have some information you might be interested in. How would you and your husband like to join me for dinner tonight?"

A face-to-face meeting. Perfect. "Actually, I was planning on calling you today," she said, not wanting him to have the upper hand. "Where would you like to meet?"

"I'm near downtown Dallas. How about the Bistro Grille on the interstate? That's about half way."

"That would be fine. Does seven-thirty sound okay?"

"Perfect," he said. "I'll see you then."

Deena could not believe she was finally going to meet this mystery man. She was anxious to call Gary but knew he would be tied up all day with clients. She looked at the magazines on the coffee table. She found one without a hunter on the front cover and mindlessly turned the pages. When it was finally time for Russell's next pill, she got a fresh bottle of water and walked into the bedroom to wake him. "Here, take this."

He sat up a little and gulped down half the water.

"I left hamburgers and potato salad in the fridge. There's also fresh milk and cereal to eat."

"Thanks, sis," he said. "You're a lifesaver. Oh, and could you feed—"

"Done. Call me later to let me know how you are."

"Will do." He gave her a weak salute.

"Oh, and you'll never believe who Gary and I are having dinner with tonight. Leon Galt—I mean, Noel Future."

Russell raised his head slightly off the pillow and opened one eye. "Really? Get me an autograph. And one for Cliff, too."

Chapter 17

"**D**o I have to wear a tie?" Gary asked when he came home and found out about the dinner plans.

"Yes. I want you to look intimidating. Also, you look so handsome when you wear a tie." She brushed the side of his salt and pepper hair.

"Too late for flattery. I'll do it for you, though." He tightened the knot around his neck. "Now what exactly is the purpose of this meeting?"

"I would assume he wants to tell us about his theory on Matthew's death. Gene Collins said Galt was determined to prove Matthew was involved in something bad. Maybe he didn't feel like he could tell Aunt Lucy and Uncle Richard directly, so he is going to tell us instead."

The beige linen pants and ivory blouse she put on was one of her favorite outfits. She wrapped her Aztec shawl over her shoulders. A turquoise brooch worked perfectly to hold it in place.

"Okay. I'm ready to go," Gary said. "You sure look pretty, Mrs. Sharpe." He took her hand and twirled her around, knocking her into the dresser.

"Ouch! My ankle!" She reached down to hold it. "I should never be allowed to wear heels." She stood up and took a deep breath.

"I'm so sorry. Are you okay?"

"I'm fine, but there are a few things I want you to remember. Don't be overly friendly. Don't let him pay for our dinner. And don't order beer."

"Why can't I order beer?"

"It makes you belch. This guy is from New York. We don't want to look like small town hicks."

"But we *are* small town hicks."

"I know, but we don't want *him* to know."

They left the bedroom, Deena slightly limping. Gary picked up his keys from the side table as well as a faded envelope off the stack of mail he had brought in earlier. "By the way, you got a letter today."

Deena looked at the name scrawled in shaky handwriting. "It's from Gran." She pulled the single folded paper out of the envelope and saw the pretty border with purple and yellow roses around the edges. She smiled remembering the rose wallpaper in Gran's old house. She read it silently and put it back in the envelope. "She thanked me for helping her. She thinks Matthew wants the truth to come out."

"Does that mean she's talking to the dead now?"

"Hey, I'll talk to you when you're dead. How is this any different?"

Gary grinned. "Because apparently her son is answering."

They drove about forty-five minutes to the restaurant. Deena was nervous. She talked about Russell and the backyard and the weather and her antique booth—obviously avoiding the subject of Matthew.

The parking lot was crowded for a Monday. "How are we going to recognize this guy?" Gary asked.

"I'll know," she said. Deena had an uncanny way of guessing people's occupations. It was probably her attention to detail. If only she could apply that same sort of attention to her own appearance.

Gary held the door, and Deena quickly scanned the waiting area. *He's not here*, she thought. Then a trim man in a perfectly tailored suit walked up to them. "Mr. and Mrs. Sharpe?"

"Yes," Deena said, wondering how he recognized them.

"I am Leon Galt." He reached out his hand, shaking Gary's first, then Deena's. "We have a table right over here." He led the way to a round table near the side of the restaurant. He pulled out Deena's chair, something Gary had stopped doing years ago.

"I took the liberty of ordering wine. I hope that's okay." Deena smiled, attempting to be gracious. He poured two more glasses. "I ordered red. I know how you Texans love your steak." He waved his hand at the various taxidermy pieces decorating the walls. Gary laughed and raised his glass in a half-toast gesture.

Deena kicked him under the table. *Ouch!* She had forgotten about her sore ankle. *I'm definitely ordering fish.*

"What do you do for a living, Gary?" Galt crossed his arms and leaned back in his chair. Deena noted his strong features and dark hair. She was surprised by his pleasantly attractive appearance, expecting him to have beady eyes and a thin mustache like the sinister villains in movies. If not an investigator or whatever he claimed to be, she would have pegged him as a history professor.

"I am a financial advisor with a company in Maycroft. And you? What do you do, Mr. Galt?"

"Please, call me Leon. I am an investigative reporter and author of numerous books."

"Anything I would have heard of?"

"Perhaps. I write under the penname of Noel Future."

Deena jumped into the conversation. "That's an unusual name. I get Noel—'Leon' spelled backwards—but why Future?"

"Because," he said with a wry smile, "my findings influence the way some events will be viewed in the future."

"What events?" Deena asked and picked up her wine glass.

"Oh, enough about me. I understand you are a retired school teacher. Journalism, I believe? That must have been fun for you." He reached over and poured more wine in her glass.

"Fun? I would describe it more as rewarding. 'If you can read, thank a teacher.'" Deena immediately regretted saying something so cliché. She could feel the blush cross her face as Gary nudged her foot under the table.

"Well then, thank you, Mrs. Sharpe," Galt said, nodding his head toward her. He grinned at her as though amused.

Before she could respond, the waiter arrived and took their order. "I'll have the baked tilapia and a glass of chardonnay." She handed her menu to the waiter and excused herself to the ladies room to regain her composure.

As she stared in the mirror, she took in deep breaths to calm her nerves. What was it about this guy that made her so unsettled? Was it because he was a successful writer and she wasn't? Was it because he was invading her territory by researching Matthew's death? She couldn't quite put her finger on it.

When she returned, the men were discussing baseball. She interrupted and said, "Let's get down to the real reason we are here, to talk about Matthew Meade."

"Of course," Galt said. He wiped his mouth with the white cloth napkin. "I understand that your family has asked you to look into the circumstances surrounding his death. Is that right?"

"Yes," Deena said. "How did you find out about that?"

"Lucy and Richard Lancaster told me. So, have you come to any conclusions thus far?"

Deena sat up in her chair. Why the heck was he asking *her* questions? She should be asking *him* questions. "Leon," she said, drawing out his name, "I think my motive is quite clear concerning my uncle's death. It is yours that is in question. Would you mind explaining why you are pokin' your nose around in my family's business?"

Gary, hating confrontation about as much as he hated the Yankees, knew the fun and games were over. Whenever Deena got serious, she talked more Southern. "Deena..."

"Of course," Galt said. "I understand your curiosity. Your uncle had been missing for fifty years. Then, out of the blue, his body is found and identified. His poor mother must be in such anguish. I am so sorry for your loss."

Deena rested her arms on the table. "Thank you, but you haven't answered my question."

"The fact of the matter is your uncle was involved in some questionable activities that led to his tragic death. Those activities are part of an extensive investigation that I have been conducting for the past five years. As a result of that investigation, I have written a manuscript that my publisher plans to take to print in the next six weeks or so. I am sure that once you read it and examine all the evidence, you will not only understand your uncle's actions but also be able to find it in your heart to forgive him for the role he played in this dreadful business." Galt sat back with the countenance of a man satisfied that he had thoroughly explained the situation.

"That's it? That's your entire explanation?" Deena asked.

Leon smiled and nodded his head.

She looked at Gary for help and then back at Galt. "Well now, you see, that dog won't hunt."

Leon, clearly confused, knitted his brow. "I beg your pardon?"

"That doesn't me anything. For starters, what 'dreadful business' are you talking about?" She made air quotes to emphasize her question.

"I am not at liberty to say. I know you have only ever published your little school newspapers, but in real publishing, there are confidentiality clauses to which an author must adhere."

Deena felt the heat rise in her neck, and this time it wasn't from a hot flash.

The waiter arrived with their meal.

"Well look at this," Gary said, trying to ease the tension. "Doesn't that look delicious? There's nothing better than a good steak. Except for fish, of course." He looked at Deena. "Yours looks wonderful, dear. Should we order you another glass of wine? Yes, let's all have some more wine."

She knew what Gary was trying to do, so she took a bite of asparagus and chewed slowly. Reaching over to pick up her glass, the fringe on her wrap dragged across her plate. She tried to wipe it off with her napkin without seeming too obvious.

At last she continued. "Leon, what was your purpose in meeting with us tonight? Obviously, you are not going to share details about your book."

"Excellent question, Mrs. Sharpe. My purpose is simply to let you know that you needn't worry yourself about investigating your uncle's death any longer. I have all the information you need, and you can read about it in a matter of months. In fact, I will personally send you an autographed copy."

Gary jumped in. "An autographed copy. That would be great. Wouldn't it, dear?"

Deena didn't take the bait. "If you were so sure of your information, then why did you talk to Deputy Simms and Gene Collins?"

"Fact-checking is an important part of any writer's research. I'm sure you know that. I was just checking to see if Mr. Collins had additional information I might be able to use."

"How did you locate Mr. Collins? And how did you happen to see him on the same day as I did?"

Galt cleared his throat.

"Were you following me?" Deena's voice got higher and louder.

"Following you? Mrs. Sharpe, you are sounding a little paranoid now."

"You didn't answer the question." It was Gary being confrontational this time. "Leon, I am afraid that the information you have provided us only raises more questions rather than answers them. I am sure you can understand our concern. I would hate to have to get our attorneys involved in this matter."

"Attorneys? No, that will not be necessary. You seem like a reasonable man, Gary. I cannot give you any details, but I will give you a general idea of the focus of my work." He looked over his shoulder and then back at them. Leaning forward as though he were revealing the U.S. nuclear codes, he whispered, "My book addresses new details about the events occurring on and around November 22, 1963, in Dallas, Texas." He sat back up in his chair.

"The Kennedy assassination?" Deena asked a little too loudly.

"*Shhh.* Yes."

"You think my uncle had something to do with *that*?" She could not hide her astonishment. "May I remind you that Matthew was killed in October of 1963."

"Not killed, disappeared. There is no evidence to prove he was killed on the day he disappeared."

Deena's mind raced. It had never occurred to her that Matthew may not have been shot on that same day. "Are you suggesting he was kidnapped or something?"

"I'm not suggesting anything in particular. I am simply telling you that I have evidence to support my conclusions. This manuscript is very detailed and includes much more information than your uncle's involvement."

"Is that so," she said.

"I had not anticipated that Matthew Meade would be found and identified just prior to the publication date. It put a wrench in my plans, I must admit. I have spent the past week making sure there are no loose ends that might cause the publisher to delay the launch date. I have found none and plan to return to New York next week after fulfilling my obligations here."

Again, with the vague responses. Deena needed to know more. "Have you tracked down Donna Morrison?" she asked, ignoring Galt's attempt at closure.

"Mrs. Sharpe, I have already said more than I should. As I told you before, you should just return home and get back to doing whatever it is you do, and you will be one of the first ones to get to read all about it."

Gary was ready to put a stop to the conversation before his wife blew a fuse. "Galt," he said, turning the name over in his head. "Wasn't there a 'Galt' who played for the White Sox back in the day?"

"I don't recall, but I know there was a Bud Sharpe who played for the Pittsburg Pirates in the early 1900s. Died young, poor fellow." Galt took a sip of wine and peered over his glass at Deena.

Was that a threat? This wouldn't be the end of her dealings with Leon Galt.

Chapter 18

"Have you tracked down Donna Morrison yet?" Leon Galt asked. He was not a patient man. "Well, keep trying." He slammed down the receiver causing the telephone in his motel room to sound like a bell ringing on a child's bicycle. He stood up and paced back and forth for a few minutes.

Finally, he pulled out his wallet and sat down. Searching through the slotted pockets, he found the right slip of paper. He dialed the number. After three rings, a man answered.

"This is Galt. I thought you were going to take care of Deena Sharpe for me. That's what I'm paying you for." He sat on the side of the bed with its tacky floral coverlet and gold fringe. "Trust me. I met with her tonight and she is definitely not planning to back off."

He waited for the man on the other end of the line to finish his list of excuses.

"I think you know how important this is to me. I am not going to let some retired teacher from Texas ruin it all. Now take care of it!"

Chapter 19

Sandra Davis loved animals so much that she chose keeping her old dog over her first husband. Good thing, too, since it turned out her Pekingese was more loyal than that no good cheatin' man. Three years later after falling for and marrying Ian, she turned her love of animals into a business. She opened the Second Chance Thrift Shop to support the local no-kill animal shelter.

Deena loved to stop in the store every chance she got to search for vintage items for her antique booth as well as to visit with her friend. Although Sandra was more than fifteen years younger, she and Deena had a lot in common and had become good friends. After the frustrating evening she had the night before, this was the perfect place for Deena to kill an hour.

"Whatcha got for me today?" Sandra asked Deena when she entered the shop carrying a bag of goodies.

"Shoes. I went through my closet today and pulled out all my heels to donate. I also have a pair of red pumps that are just too young for me." Deena set the bag on the counter and walked over to a chair Sandra kept at the front of the shop for visitors.

"Are you limping?"

"Yes. I hit my ankle on the dresser when Gary was pushing me around." She saw the wide-eyed look on her friend's face. "Not like that," she said. "Gary thought it would be fun to ball-room dance in the bedroom."

"You worried me there for a second," she said and walked back to the storeroom to set down Deena's bag. She returned and sat behind the counter on her padded stool. "Speaking of dancing, we missed you two at the Pets & Patriots Ball. We brought in quite of bit of money for the shelter, though."

"Things have just been a little crazy with this family stuff. We'll go to the fall event, I promise."

The shop door opened, jingling the bell Sandra kept tied to the handle. A man and woman, obviously tourists, walked in. Sandra greeted them, and then leaned over to Deena and whispered, "If you're shopping today, you might want to check out the glass aisle. There's some new pottery over there."

Deena got up and went straight to her favorite section. She immediately spotted two pieces she knew were of good quality. The first was an orange Blenko glass decanter. She had sold similar ones in her booth before. The other was an aqua vase with a matte finish. She picked it up and turned it over, hoping to see the name of her favorite Colorado pottery. Bingo! Van Briggle. She carried the pieces to the front counter and winked at her friend.

One of the things Deena liked about shopping at thrift stores and antique malls was the chance it gave her to stroll down memory lane. She would see an old cross-stitch picture or a set of china and think, "My mother used to have that." Occasionally, she bought something simply because she had once had it as a child. Gary would look at the tattered lunch box or Ponytail vinyl 45-record holder and know she was trying to re-capture that feeling—the one you get when suddenly thrust into another time or place by a memory. After a few months, the items would find their way into the booth or back to the thrift shop. Deena referred to re-donating these items as "renting memories."

Scanning the housewares, she spotted a vintage avocado-green crockpot like the one she got years ago as a wedding gift. It made her smile even though she knew it was not something that would sell in her booth. She picked up a teak-covered ice bucket from the sixties but put it back when she saw the inside liner was cracked. Deena had several pieces of vintage art in her booth and saw the tourist couple looking through the stack of pictures. When they walked away, she went over and picked up a vintage framed paint-by-numbers picture of a circus scene. She knew it was kitschy, but those pictures always sold in her booth.

"You know you have these pieces underpriced," Deena said and set her final item on the counter.

"I know, but that's how I get people like you to keep coming in to find the treasures. And sometimes they buy the junk, like this ugly clown picture."

They shared a laugh.

Deena set her purse on the counter. Pulling out her billfold, the picture of Matthew with the girl fell out. Sandra picked it up.

"I love these black-and-white pictures from the Sixties," she said. "I wish those dresses were back in style. Do you think I would look good with a bouffant?" She held the picture next to her face.

"Absolutely. I'm sure Kristy could fix you right up." She handed her credit card to Sandra and put the picture back in her purse.

"I'll remember that if I ever take a *third* engagement picture."

"Why did you call it an engagement picture?"

"That's what I thought the picture was," Sandra said. "I'm just guessing."

Deena pulled it back out, and Sandra pointed to the girl's hand. "See how she has her hand posed to show off her ring?"

"I hadn't noticed that," Deena said. She looked at the picture more closely. "Hmm. That changes things."

She had no idea that Matthew had been engaged. Could this be another clue to his cause of death? Anything seemed more likely than Galt's wild theory about Matthew's involvement in the Kennedy assassination. It was time to track down this mystery fiancé.

Chapter 20

Working in his office was rare for Trey Simms these days. The Bingham County Sheriff's Department had a big drug case with the ATF and most of the deputies were in the field. Simms stopped by to fill out some paperwork before heading home for the day. He went by the front desk to pick up his messages from Renee.

"*Please* call Henry Wilcox," she said. "He has called at least five times in the last two days."

"Who is he? What does he want?"

"I don't know, but he says he can only talk to you."

Simms headed to his office and unlocked the door. Something made a shuffling noise near his desk. He put his hand on his pistol. Turning on the light, he glimpsed a mouse leaping off the desk and escaping behind a file cabinet. He spied the half-eaten bag of crackers left there since Monday. He threw them out and dialed the number for Henry Wilcox. The man on the other end answered on the first ring.

"This is Deputy Simms. What can I do for you?"

"I wanted to talk to you about that murder case. Matthew Meade. In the paper it said to call you if anybody had information. Well, I got some information."

Simms was surprised. He hadn't expected to hear anything about the case, especially after a month had gone by since the news was released. "What information do you have, sir?"

"It's about some of the goings on at his place of business. Some illegal stuff you know. And there's more."

"I'm all ears." Trey leaned back in his chair waiting for some wild story about inter-office politics.

"This ain't the sort of thing I can talk about over the phone. I think you need to hear it in person."

Simms tapped his pen on the notepad in front of him. His in-laws were coming for dinner and his wife would kill him if he got home late. At least half an hour of paperwork was staring him in the face. "Just a minute," he said. He put the line on hold and called the sheriff's secretary. "Is he in?"

"Yes. I'll connect you."

Simms explained the situation to his boss.

Sheriff Long was clear. "Look Simms, we don't have time to chase rabbits right now. Tell this guy to come in and make a statement. If there is anything there, we can follow up. Hey, ask him if he wants you to put him in touch with the family. That might keep him out of our hair for a while."

Simms switched back over to the other line. "Mr. Wilcox. I am not going to be able to meet with you for a week or so. You are welcome to come down to the office and submit a statement. The other thing I can do is put you in touch with the Meade family if both of you are willing. They are very anxious to learn any new information." He held his breath.

"Well, they might not like what I have to say, but they probably need to hear it," Wilcox grumbled.

"Fine. Fine," Simms said. "I'll get in touch with them and give them your number. If they are interested, they will give you a call."

He hung up thinking, *This won't be the only murder case around here if I don't get home soon.*

Chapter 21

Russell was more than happy to go with Deena to meet Henry Wilcox. Gary insisted that she not go alone even though they were meeting in a public place. Frankly, she did not want to go alone either.

"This is real Watergate stuff," Russell said, getting in Deena's car. "It's like we're going to meet Deep Throat."

She recognized the Tommy Bahama shirt he had on as one she gave him for Christmas. "Yes, except that we are meeting him in a restaurant and not a parking garage. Oh, and we are going to Dallas, not D.C."

"Kill joy. It's still pretty exciting."

Deena turned to look back over her shoulder before pulling onto the highway. Russell reached into his pocket and slipped something into the glove compartment. He adjusted the air vents on the dash and pointed them right on his face. "When are we going to get some rain? It's not even noon and it's already boiling outside."

The Texas heat was brutal. Stepping out in the midday sun was like standing too close to the fireplace, the heat cooking your skin in minutes, the beads of sweat drying up almost as soon as they sprang from your pores.

Russell crossed his arms and settled in for the drive. "What did this guy say he wants to tell you?"

"I've told you all I know. He says he has information about the medical supply company where Uncle Matthew worked. He also has dirt on people who worked there. Thinks it may be connected to the murder. You will know as much as I do as soon as we get there."

Russell was like a kid on his way to Disneyland. Deena half expected him to ask, *Are we there yet?* Inside, she was just as excited as he was, but she was trying to play it cool. After their dinner with Leon Galt, she was anxious to find out as much as she could about her uncle's history. Galt seemed so sure of his information and equally anxious for her to stop nosing around, which just added more kindling to the cook stove.

She decided not to say anything to Lucy and Richard about the accusations until her next visit. You don't exactly call someone up and say, "Oh by the way, your brother may have been involved in one of the most notorious crimes of the twentieth century. Have a nice day."

"Where is this place?" Russell asked, as they got closer to downtown.

"It's in Oak Cliff. Not too much farther. By the way, let me do the talking. We don't want to reveal too much in case this guy is just a screwball."

"Hey. Screwballs are people, too."

After several turns and a few turn-arounds, they parked in front of a barbeque joint that looked older than dirt and just about as clean. These were usually the best places to find great home cooking. The sweet, smoky smell permeated the air, even in the car.

They went in to find a few tables filled with men in jeans and t-shirts licking thick, red sauce off their fingers and guzzling large glasses of iced tea. One older man sat alone in the corner and motioned for them to join him.

"I'm Henry," he said, wiping his hands on his napkin.

A handshake was out of the question. "I'm Deena and this is my brother, Russell."

"Glad to meet you. Why don't you order your lunch then come back and we'll have a talk. I recommend the pork ribs. Best you'll ever put in your mouth."

Deena headed to the counter to order. "Seems normal enough," she whispered to Russell. She ordered a barbeque beef sandwich with dill pickles. Russell chose the pork ribs and barbequed beans. They picked up their cups of tea and went over to join their host.

"It's another scorcher out there." Russell took several napkins out of the metal holder and wiped his forehead.

"You bet it is, but I don't think any of us are here to talk about the weather." Henry scooped out the last bite of potato salad from the paper cup. He wiped his mouth and hands and pushed his empty plate away from him. "What I have to say may not make you happy, but it's the honest truth. I've waited fifty years to tell someone this story. I don't care if you believe it or not, but it's the truth."

"Why haven't you told anyone before now?" Deena asked.

"Let me just start at the beginning and then you'll see." A waitress brought over the order and set it on the table. Deena and her brother began eating as they listened to the old man's story.

"I started working at Barnes Medical Supply in 1963. I was just twenty-two and worked in the accounts department. Meade was a manager. He had a friend by the name of Gene Collins who worked in the warehouse. I had only been there a couple of months, but I started noticing some discrepancies with the books. Seems like there was more merchandise going out than there was money coming in. Being new, I wasn't sure what to do about it. I told my supervisor who told me to mind my own business, or I'd be out of a job." He drank the end of his iced tea and set the cup on the table.

"I began to suspect there was some funny business going on, and it was happening in the warehouse. Collins was the head honcho back there, so I figured he was the ringleader. What I didn't know was that he and Matthew Meade were army buddies and that Meade had gotten him that job. I was young and green and thought I was doing the right thing. Everyone thought highly of your uncle and said he was a good guy. I decided to tell him about my suspicions. He said he would check into it. That was about a week before he disappeared."

Deena and Russell hung on every word. She set down her sandwich and wiped barbeque sauce from her mouth. "Then what happened?"

"I was at the Park Street Café the next Wednesday when Meade, Collins, and this woman named Donna Morrison came in. I was sitting with my wife on the opposite side of the cafe. When I saw them, I switched places with my wife so that they wouldn't see me. I didn't want to have to speak to them, you know. Donna was a secretary for the shipping department.

Seeing them all buddied up like that, I figured she was in on it, too."

"In on what?" Deena asked.

"Hold your horses. I'm getting there."

Henry Wilcox had waited many years to tell his story. He'd probably rehearsed it in his head over and over. He was going to tell it his own way.

"The missus and I had to sit there awhile waiting for them to leave. They finished eating and Gene gets up and heads around the back by the kitchen. A minute later, Donna stands up and goes flying out of the place—that's how my wife described it to me. I could see Gene over my shoulder. He goes to the pay phone and makes a call. Then he heads back to the table and they pay their checks and leave. Apparently, it wasn't long after that when someone shot and killed Mr. Meade."

Deena thought about what Gene had told her and wondered why their stories differed. "Are you sure Gene Collins went to the pay phone and not to the men's room?"

"You bet I am. He made a phone call. If you ask me, he was calling one of his boys to tell him when and where to find Meade."

Russell looked puzzled and asked, "You think the warehouse guys killed him because he was going to blow the whistle on their stolen merchandise racket?"

Henry nodded excitedly. "That's exactly what I think."

"Why didn't you tell the sheriff's office your suspicions when Matthew disappeared?" Deena asked.

"I saw what happened to your uncle. I knew just to keep my mouth shut and mind my own business. A week later, management got wise to the scam and fired the whole lot of them, including Donna Morrison and everyone in the warehouse."

Deena wasn't sure what to think about the story. "You say Donna was fired a week later? Did she stay in Maycroft?"

"I heard she moved up to Oklahoma."

Deena eyed the stranger as if buying a used car, looking for holes in his story. "Did the company ever acknowledge a connection between the two events?"

"No, but they weren't there that night at the diner. They didn't see what I saw."

"How much longer did you work there?" Russell asked.

"I quit about six months later when my wife wanted to move here to Dallas."

"I'm not saying I don't believe you," Deena said, "but do you have any proof to back this up?"

"I got my gut, and my gut tells me that's what happened."

"What about Donna Morrison? Do you know anything else about her?"

"She seemed nice enough. Very pretty. I didn't really know her. The guys in the warehouse stayed away from her because she said her boyfriend was the jealous type and would come after them if they tried anything. Just gossip."

Reaching into her purse, Deena pulled out the photo of Matthew and his fiancé she had been carrying around. "Do you recognize this girl?"

Henry took the photo and pushed his glasses up higher on his nose. "Nope. Can't say that I do." He handed it back to Deena.

"Do you have the names of anyone else who worked at the company?" Deena was hoping to find someone to corroborate his story.

"Nope, and I wouldn't tell you if I did. I only mentioned Collins and Morrison because their names were in the newspaper back when it first happened. It said they were the last two people to see Mr. Meade alive. I'm number three."

Deena looked at Russell and back at Henry. "I can't tell you how much I appreciate your talking to us today. I can promise you that I will follow up on this information."

"I'd thank you kindly to leave my name out of it on account of what happened to your uncle."

"Of course," Deena said. She excused herself to the ladies room to wash up. When she returned, Henry was gone.

"We picked up his check," Russell said. "I hope that was okay."

"Sure. I'll pay you back."

"Forget it. It's on me."

"Literally, it's on you," she said, pointing to the sauce that had dripped onto his shirt.

"Ahh. It was worth it. Best barbeque I ever had. And what about that story? You've got to fill me in on the details about all this on the drive home."

They filled their cups with more tea, and Deena wrapped up her half-eaten sandwich.

As they drove home, Deena started from the beginning, from when she first went to see Aunt Lucy and Uncle Richard. She told him how Gran was mostly confined to the bed and had dreamed she saw Matthew in her room. Trying to remember as many details as possible, she told him about her meeting with Deputy Simms, the church ladies, and Gene Collins.

"So, you're saying that Collins gave the exact same story as Henry, except for the pay phone part? That seems like a pretty big difference if he were calling people to take out Matthew."

"I agree," Deena said. "But I find it hard to believe that Gene Collins would have his army buddy—the friend who gave him a job—murdered for something like that."

"Maybe Collins was being pressured by others. Maybe he didn't know they were going to kill him. They might have planned just to rough him up and scare him but something went wrong." Russell leaned back in his seat. "Henry Wilcox may not have been right about the murder, but he was definitely right about those killer ribs."

"Do you want to hear about our dinner with Leon Galt, alias Noel Future?"

"I totally forgot about that! I was so drugged on my medication that I completely forgot. Did you get his autograph, by the way?"

Deena looked over at her brother in the passenger seat and glared. "Just wait until you hear what he said."

She described his arrogant attitude—especially toward Texans—wanting Russell to dislike him as much as she did. She obviously had a bone to pick and finally got down to the marrow. "He said he was about to publish a book about the JFK assassination and that Uncle Matthew was involved." She glanced over at her brother's face for a reaction.

His mouth gaped and his eyes widened. "Do you think that's possible?"

Deena was not sure if her brother was excited or appalled. "That's ridiculous, right?"

"Of course, but it's intriguing. Noel Future has researched and published some compelling stuff on all kinds of topics. The fact that he would even make this claim is really something."

"He did not offer even one shred of evidence, by the way. Said we could read all about it in his new book. I don't trust him as far as I could pitch him."

"If he didn't back it up, what was his point in telling you about it?"

Deena exited the highway to take the road to Crossbow. "Gary and I wondered the same thing. We decided his main point was to tell me to stop my investigation. He acted like he was doing me a favor."

"That actually makes sense. As soon as one of these conspiracy books is released, it starts a firestorm of blow back. Everybody and his dog wants to prove why parts of the theory, or even the whole thing, is wrong. The conspiracy community goes nuts with speculation."

Deena rolled her eyes at the thought. "Sounds like good publicity for a new book."

Russell shook his head. "Absolutely. And Noel Future is a master at it. He'll be on television, in magazines, at book signings—you name it."

"So, whether what he says is true or not, he will end up making a lot of money."

"Yep, Noel 'Fortune.'"

Turning down the road toward Russell's house, Deena was outraged by the very idea of someone making blood money off their uncle's death. "What about the publisher? Wouldn't they worry about lawsuits if what he says is proven false?"

"I'm sure they're careful. That's probably why he wants you to stop your investigation. If you find out what really happened to Uncle Matthew, the publisher will probably back out of the deal."

"Good point. Right now, our only theory is Henry's. As much as I would hate for it to be true, we may need to make a case for it just to stop Galt from publishing." She stopped the car in the driveway. "I really need to find out what Galt is specifically claiming about Matthew's involvement in the assassination."

"That was eight years after he left the military, right? Didn't you say Collins called Matthew a sharpshooter?"

"Yes. So did Deputy Simms. Collins said he did 'wet work.'"

"Wet work?" Russell seemed astonished. "You mean like sniper stuff?"

"I think that's was he meant." She turned in her seat to face her brother. "You don't think he's saying Matthew was part of the assassination itself, do you? Please, for Pete's sake, say no."

Russell sat silently. Despite the searing heat, Deena suddenly felt a cold chill.

* * *

MAGGIE SCRATCHED AND howled on the other side of the door ready for Russell to come in. He stepped in the doorway and squatted to scratch her neck. Catching a glimpse of someone standing in his kitchen, he fell backward on the floor. "Geez!"

Cliff stepped out from the kitchen and waved to Russell. He was talking on the telephone that hung from the kitchen wall. He shook his head and mumbled something Russell couldn't hear and then hung up.

"Sorry, man. Didn't mean to scare you. My air-conditioner is on the fritz, and I didn't think you'd mind me hanging out here until the repairman comes. I used the key under the garden gnome."

"No problem. I just didn't expect to see anyone in here." Russell stood back up. "Hey, didn't you install that air conditioner? We used to fix systems like that all the time."

"It needed a part. Couldn't find anything to rig it with."

Russell walked over to the sliding glass door to let Maggie out. He picked up the key Cliff had set on the counter, taking it outside to return it to its hiding place. Cliff walked out behind him.

"They should be here any minute. I'm going to wait at my house."

As he walked toward the connecting gate, Russell asked, "Who was on the phone?"

"Sales call."

The large plastic bowl that Maggie drank from outside was empty, so Russell got the hose to refill it. He put the nozzle to his mouth for a drink then spat the water out on the ground. "Hot," he grumbled. He went back into the house and walked down the hallway toward his room, not noticing something out of place as he passed the second bedroom. The door of the gun safe, always kept shut, was slightly ajar.

Chapter 22

The developer who built Butterfly Gardens, the subdivision where Deena and Gary lived, was an amateur entomologist who chose insect names for streets rather than the usual tree or bird names. Residents of Maycroft poked fun at the area at first but could not resist the open floor plans and large lots. However, when he tried to name a street "Boll Weevil," the city council had to intervene.

Deena lived on Cricket Lane, just down from June Bug Drive. As she turned the corner on the way home from dropping off Russell, she was surprised to see an unfamiliar car parked in front of her house. Someone was sitting inside. She was surprised the neighborhood watch wasn't out in full force. Despite all their drama, people in the suburbs could be awfully protective when it came to the safety of their neighbors. She pressed the garage door opener and pulled into the driveway.

The driver waited and then got out of the car.

That's when Deena recognized her cousin. "Mark! What on earth are you doing here? Is something wrong? Is it Gran?"

"No, nothing like that," he said as he walked up to her. "I was just in the area and thought I would stop by."

"Come on in." They entered the house through the garage, and Deena set her purse and keys on the entry table. "This is a nice surprise. I wish you had called. I was at your parents' house just the other day. Have you been waiting long?"

"No, not that long."

Deena could tell by the sweat on his face and shirt that it had been longer than he was letting on. Mark took more after his father, Uncle Richard, than his mother's side of the family. He had dark eyes and curly brown hair that he used to wear tied back in a ponytail in the seventies. Nowadays he kept it short despite the ever-enlarging bald spot.

"Oh dear," Deena said when she spotted the piles of papers in the middle of the den floor. She walked over to close the double doors to hide the mess. "Let me just shut these. I've been going through all the papers and stuff I got from your folks."

"Would you mind if I have a look?" Mark took several steps toward the door. "I'm curious to see what all was in those boxes."

"Well, sure. But you must be burning up. Would you like some water or iced tea?"

"Iced tea would be great." Mark stepped into the den and stood over the piles.

Deena got two glasses down from the cabinet and filled them with ice from her refrigerator door. She pulled out a pitcher of tea and filled the glasses. "Sweetened or unsweetened?" she called out from the kitchen.

"Sweetened."

She picked up the sugar bowl, stirred a generous amount into each glass, and carried them into the office. "Nothing like a glass of sweet tea on hot day to wet your whistle." Mark, leaning over a pile of letters and documents, quickly stood up.

"See anything interesting?" She took a sip from her own glass as she handed the other to Mark.

"No, no," he said. "Just looking."

She set her glass on the desk. "Here are some pictures of Matthew. Maybe you know some of the people he's with." Moving a stack of mail over to the side, she put the photos in the middle of the desk. "Why don't you sit here and have a look." She turned on the desk lamp and motioned to the chair.

"Thanks." He took several big gulps of tea, put down his glass, and sat in Deena's rolling desk chair. "Have you found anything out about his death?" Mark squinted, trying to make out the faces in the fuzzy black-and-white pictures.

"Not really. I'm still trying to put the pieces of the puzzle together." She did not want to say anything that might cause him to worry, so she didn't mention her conversations with Leon Galt or Henry Wilcox.

He shuffled through the photographs. "These are some of the cousins on my father's side." He handed her the photo.

Deena picked up a ballpoint pen and labelled the back. "Do you know their names?"

"I can't remember." He handed her another picture. "These are people from our church."

Could this be Harriet or her friends? Deena continued making notes on the pictures. When her hands were full, she set them on the stack of mail, causing it to topple to the floor.

"I'll get that," Mark said and he bent down to retrieve the letters. For a moment, he froze, doubled over in the chair. When he sat up, his face was a ghostly white.

"Are you okay? Did you get dizzy?"

"No. Yes, I'm fine."

"Come on into the living room. This room gets all the afternoon sun. I'll get you some more tea." Picking up his glass, she stood by the door, waiting for him, worried he might be unsteady from leaning over.

He got up and followed her out. She went straight to the refrigerator and pulled out the pitcher of tea. "I do have another picture in my purse I want to show you, though."

When she turned around, he was standing by the front door with his hand on the knob. "I've got to go. I forgot I have to get back. Thanks for the tea."

Deena worried something was wrong. "Are you sure? Gary will be home in—" Before she could finish her sentence, he left. She walked to the front window and watched him get in his car and drive off. How strange. Mark was her only cousin on her mother's side of the family, and he was several years younger. Could it have been his blood sugar? She walked back to the den to get her glass. That's when she noticed the letter from Gran—purple roses and all—laying on top of the stack of mail. Could that have spooked Mark?

When Gary walked through the door after work, Deena was sitting in the middle of the floor surrounded by the sorted stacks of papers and pictures. She looked like a daisy and the stacks were her petals. "Don't stop me now," she said when Gary poked his head in the door to greet her. "I only have this last bunch to sort and I'm done."

He returned after a few minutes wearing shorts and sandals, carefully stepping over the piles to sit in the desk chair.

"There. That's it," she said, standing up to stretch. She sat down in the easy chair to admire her work.

"Congratulations. What's in all the stacks?" As a type-A financial wizard, he appreciated a good sorting system.

"I have this small stack of photos of Matthew when he was older. The other big stack has all the pictures I don't think are important. Then there are military papers, legal documents, and other papers belonging to Gran that seem irrelevant. That huge stack has postcards, letters, greeting cards, and such. It will take me awhile to get through all those." She put her hand on the last stack. "And these are report cards, school certificates, and things that really don't involve the case."

"Nice job. Does that mean we can pick up some of this mess?"

Deena knew he was dying to clean the place up. "Sure. I only have to deal with those few photos and the correspondence. Let's put the rest back in the boxes." She picked up the pictures and put them on the desk. Gary helped her with the rest.

"Guess who was here today?" Not waiting for an answer, she said, "Mark Lancaster."

"Lucy and Richard's Mark?"

"Yes. When I got back from Oak Cliff, he was sitting in his car outside the house." She told him about the strange visit.

"Maybe you should call later tonight and check on him."

"I don't have his phone number, but I'll call Aunt Lucy tomorrow. I was going to call her anyway because I want to drive back up there and talk to her and Gran."

Gary stacked the boxes in the corner under the window. "I want to hear all about your meeting with this guy today."

"If his story turns out to be true, we may have figured out the mystery."

"Can you tell me about it while we eat?" Gary asked. "I'm starving."

"You fire up the grill, and I'll get the chicken ready."

It was too hot out to eat on the patio, so they sat at the kitchen table. Deena, still full from lunch, pushed food around her plate as she described the meeting with Wilcox.

"Do you think this guy is legit?"

"I think he truly believes what he told us. He doesn't seem to have a motive to lie. I think the part about stealing from the warehouse probably happened, but I'm just not sure someone would kill Matthew because of it."

"That would seem to require a big leap of logic. What do you plan to ask Gran?"

"I want to know as much as I can about Matthew's army and work experience. Russell said that if there is no other reasonable explanation for the murder, Leon Galt is free to say just about anything he wants." She swirled the ice around in her glass.

"Speaking of that, I talked to one of our lawyers at work today. You've met Scott Myers, right? I gave him a short synopsis of the situation, minus the JFK part. He said that once Gran dies, no one else in the family would really have a case to sue Galt for libel unless they were directly implicated." He looked at Deena. "That means the clock is ticking."

"The clock was already ticking because of Galt's book."

The phone rang, and Deena got up to answer it.

Gary set about cleaning up the dishes and was just finishing up when she returned. "That was Russell," she said. "Seems like

Galt was telling the truth about having other obligations in Dallas. He is going to be signing books at a shop outside the Sixth Floor Museum on Saturday."

"His new book?"

"No, his CIA book. Russell wants to go, and I haven't been there in ages. It might be interesting. What do you think?"

Gary scratched his head. "Umm, one problem. Texas is playing the Yankees Saturday night, and Scott invited me to the game. I can cancel if you want me to."

"No, that's fine. Russell and I can go. You try to catch a foul ball, and I'll try to catch a killer."

Chapter 23

Now that she was no longer a working gal, Deena could not keep making excuses about the clutter in her car. The cargo area of the SUV was a travelogue of her life, reflecting her appearance, adventures, habits, correspondence, and even culinary choices. It might have stayed that way a few more months had it not been for the leftover barbeque sandwich that had made its way under the passenger seat. The stench, much like the port-a-potties at the beach, blasted her senses when she opened the car door to retrieve her sunglasses.

"Oh, lordy," she said, slamming the door shut. "Gary is going to kill me." He was one of those men who took his car as seriously as he took his finances. He liked to say, "Take care of it, and it will take care of you." She decided to back it out into the driveway and leave the doors open while she pulled out the contents. Hopefully, her nosy neighbors weren't watching.

Dragging a garbage can up to the door, the autopsy began. A pair of shoes, a winter scarf, a broken umbrella, empty soda cans, potato chip bags, three Sharpies, seven pens, newspapers, one glove, and finally, the barbeque sandwich. She was surprised there wasn't a family of mice living in there.

The car was hot as coal, but at least it looked more presentable. A half a can of Lysol later, it was suitable for driving. Knowing she was running late, she opted not to go by the store on the way to Lucy and Richard's. They would understand if she showed up empty handed this time. After all, she was family.

The drive seemed shorter, probably because she had a lot on her mind.

Just as before, Lucy had prepared sandwiches, iced tea, and a plate of sugar cookies. Richard was reading a fishing magazine, and Gran was sitting at the kitchen table waiting for her.

"Gran," Deena said, "I'm so glad to see you."

"Oh sweetie, give me some sugar." Gran reached up and wrapped her arms around Deena's neck. "How are you?"

"I'm just fine. You look good. Russell and Gary send their love."

Sitting around the table reminded Deena of the old days when her mother would take the family on holidays for visits. She was suddenly back in her pleated, plaid dress and black velvet Mary Janes, listening to the grown-ups, leaning on her mother's arm. An ache, deep inside, reminded her that life was like the snapshots she had brought with her, one memory captured at a time.

"Deena, dear, aren't you hungry?" Lucy asked. "Maybe you need some iced tea to cool down."

"Yes, that's what I need," she answered politely, remembering she had said the same thing to Lucy's son. "By the way, how is Mark. Is he feeling better?"

"What do you mean?" Richard walked over to rotate the small countertop fan toward the kitchen table.

"When he came by the house yesterday, he seemed a little dizzy. He left in a hurry, and I thought he might be sick."

"That's odd," Richard said. "He didn't say a word to us about driving to Maycroft. Let's go into the front room where it will be more comfortable." He helped Gran out of her chair.

When they were all settled, Gran started right in asking Deena questions. "Have you been able to find out anything about Matthew? Have you found out who took his life?"

Deena was surprised by her directness, expecting tears and tales of midnight apparitions. "I'm following two different leads. I have several questions, but first I have these pictures to show you." She pulled out three photographs. "I'm hoping you might recognize the people in them." The first one was of Matthew in his army uniform standing next to two other soldiers.

"Isn't he handsome?" Gran held the picture in her trembling hands. "I still have that uniform in the cedar chest. This was taken shortly after boot camp." Moving the picture forward and backward to get just the right focus, she said, "That boy on the left is Bill Barnett. They lived next door. I don't know who that other boy is."

Deena made a note on the back and passed it to Lucy and Richard who shook their heads, confirming they did not know the identity of the other person either. She handed Gran the second photo, showing Matthew leaning against a blue Chevy and standing next to a man and woman.

"That's when he got his new car," Gran crooned. "He was so proud of it. That's Jackie and Ed. Now, what was their last name? I can't remember right off hand. Matthew lived in a garage apartment at their house for about a year after he got his discharge. They were nice folks and took good care of him in Maycroft."

The last picture was the one that Sandra said looked like an engagement photo. "This is the last one."

"Oh yes," Gran said. "Katherine. She was such a pretty little thing. My, my. I haven't seen this picture in years."

"She and Matthew look to be pretty close. Were they engaged?"

"Yes. Engaged to be married. Katherine Clark." Gran fell silent. Perhaps she was dreaming of what might have been if only Matthew had stayed with her.

Deena interrupted her granmother's thoughts. "What happened to them?"

"Matthew called it off. I know he loved her, but he said he didn't want to marry her."

"Did he tell you why he called it off?"

"He said it was to protect her. That's the same reason he gave for leaving Bingham—to protect his papa and me."

Lucy stood up and came over to look at the picture. "Did he say what he was protecting you from?" she asked.

"Ghosts," Gran said. "Ghosts from his past in the army. That's all he would say."

Deena took the picture and wrote Katherine's name on the back. "Do you know what happened to her after that?"

"We heard she married a rancher and moved to West Texas. Matthew would say, 'Oh Mama, don't worry about me. You and Papa are all the family I need.'"

Deena studied the three photographs. "What can you tell me about his service in the army?"

"They gave him a lot of important assignments. He talked to his papa about it some, but they never would tell me. Frank said it would upset me too much. I always wondered if that was why Matthew disappeared—that maybe he was hiding from someone. We hired a private detective, you know, but he never found anything." She took a breath. "Now, I know that my son was dead all along."

Deena knew her grandmother was emotional, but it was, after all, her wish to find out the truth. "Right before he went missing, did he mention anything unusual going on at work?"

"No. He liked his job and said he had some friends there. We hadn't talked to him in about a month before he went missing. If only..."

Deena waited a minute for Gran to regain her composure. "Do you know the names of any of the people he worked with?"

"He had an address book. It's in the cedar chest. Richard, help me up and I'll get it."

Leaning on her cane and Deena's arm, Gran shuffled into the bedroom and sat in a straight-back chair next to the old wooden chest.

Richard lifted the hinged lid and stepped back out of the way. The acrid smell of mothballs cleansed their sinuses.

Gran gently pushed aside items on top to reach the bottom. "Here it is," she said and pulled out a small black book with yellowed edges. She held it out for Deena. "Please don't lose this, dear."

"I'll take good care of it, I promise."

Gran, tired from the visit, said she wanted to lie down for a spell. Deena said her goodbyes and promised to return as soon as she had news to report. They went back to the kitchen where Lucy refilled their empty glasses.

Lucy and Richard looked at Deena expectantly.

"I have a lead that is related to Matthew's job," Deena said softly. "It seems a little far-fetched, but right now it's all I've got." She filled them in on some of the details. "And another thing, I met with Leon Galt."

"Leon Galt? For heaven's sake." Lucy clutched the edge of the table. "Is that the man who came by here asking all those questions?"

"Yes. You talked to him recently, right? You told him I was investigating the murder."

"We haven't seen or heard from that man since his first visit," Lucy said, her eyes full of fear, "Oh my, I hope he isn't stirring up any trouble."

"Don't worry," Deena said, trying to sound reassuring. "I have talked to him and everything is fine. He is just interested in the case." There she went lying to old people again.

"You know," Lucy said, "maybe Mark talked to Mr. Galt. Richard, I remember you showed him that man's business card."

Deena reached for her purse. "Can I have Mark's phone number? I'd like to call him myself."

Her cousin Mark, she decided, apparently had as many secrets as the mysterious Leon Galt.

Chapter 24

Selling found treasures, whether online, at a flea market, or in a store, allowed a shopaholic to drink the wine without getting drunk. The thrill of the hunt, the power of possession—all thirsts quenched without any of the bitter after-taste. Buy, own, sell, repeat. The perfect diet requiring no self-control.

Even Gary supported Deena's entrepreneurial endeavors. Fewer knick-knacks sitting around meant more room for an even bigger big-screen TV. Circle of life, he called it.

With inventory piling up in the guest room, Deena knew she had neglected her booth long enough. She opened the door, and projects put off until summer glared at her with their unfinished surfaces and not-yet repaired parts dangling like broken limbs from a tree. Not today, she thought, brushing past the bigger pieces in favor of some smaller items. She wrapped newspaper around the breakables, carefully placing them in plastic crates she could easily carry into the antique mall.

After almost an hour, her treasures were tagged and ready to go in search of new homes. Hopefully, rich people's homes. After placing the crates in the car, she picked up her small kit filled with pins and pens, nails and knobs, bits and bobs—everything she might need to organize her small booth space.

Texans rarely throw a fit when they get mad; they throw a *hissy* fit. That was Deena's first inclination when she saw her booth in total disarray. The regulars who frequented the mall throughout the year were careful with collectibles that filled the shelves and hung from the walls. The summer tourists, however, treated shopping like dumpster diving, tossing merchandise here and there with no regard for its value.

Deena spent a good fifteen minutes taking items that belonged to other dealers up to the front desk to be returned to their rightful spaces. In the process, she found several broken items that had to be tossed.

Each piece of glass and pottery had to be dusted separately and placed carefully to catch the best light and a potential customer's eye. Deena liked to put little cards in front her special pieces with the maker's name, such as Roseville, McCoy, and Weller. Gary often teased her, saying she enjoyed displaying her collectibles more than selling them.

"What a pretty piece."

She looked around to find Rhonda Pryor admiring her newly acquired Blenko decanter.

"Hi Rhonda. Looking for anything special today?"

"You know, if something speaks to me, I may have to buy it." She picked up a cloisonné vase to read the price on the bottom and set it back in place. "Lloyd tells me you want to work for the newspaper."

"I talked to him earlier in the summer about a job." Deena turned her face and sneezed. "Sorry...dust. I have been busy since then trying to find out information about my uncle's murder."

"Murder?" Rhonda repeated. "That's not a word you hear very often in Maycroft."

"Do you remember about a month ago when the Dallas paper ran a story and picture of a John Doe who was killed fifty years ago?"

Rhonda remembered the article and nodded. "Oh sure. It was someone from Bingham."

"That was my uncle. I'm trying to unravel the mystery about what happened to him and how he died."

"That's just the kind of story that sells newspapers. Do you mind if I tell Lloyd about it?"

"Not at all. I haven't written anything yet because there are still so many unanswered questions."

"Well, good luck with your booth and with your story."

After Rhonda left, Deena felt a new sense of excitement. She got pen and paper from her kit and wrote a to-do list: call Mark, talk to Collins, research Barnes Medical Supply, call Matthew's phone list, find Donna Morrison. She put a star next to the last entry. She had a hunch that Donna could prove helpful—if she were still alive, that is.

Chapter 25

When Deena picked up Russell at his house on Saturday morning, he was red as a fire ant. She couldn't help but feel sorry for him as he inched and ouched his way into the passenger seat of her car.

"What happened to you?" she asked, wondering if he would survive their trip over to Dallas.

"I fell asleep in Cliff's pool." He pulled down the visor to survey his face.

"You mean the bunker?"

He shook his head and let out a groan. "In the water. It's too hot out. We'll have to come up with plan B for the bunker."

"That sun can be deadly, you know. Be sure to wear sunscreen." Russell turned his head slowly and gave his little sister a snarky look. "Thanks. I hadn't thought of that."

On the drive to downtown Dallas, Deena recounted her visit to Gran's, including the part about Mark. She wanted to see if Russell found it as suspicious as she did.

"You definitely need to talk to Mark. Maybe that's how Leon Galt found out about your investigation. I always thought Mark was a little slimy. Always looking out for himself."

The parking lot next to the Sixth Floor Museum was pickle packed, so Deena circled a few times waiting for someone to leave. She finally found a spot and watched her brother carefully get out of the car. "Are you going to make it?" she asked.

"I survived combat duty. I can survive a little sunburn."

Walking toward the front entrance, she noticed he was carrying something bulky in the pocket of his shorts. "I can put whatever it is in my handbag if that would help."

"I got it," he said, sticking his hand protectively in his pocket. He walked up the steps to the museum entrance and held open the door.

Before entering, Deena looked up at the building. Like most things from childhood, she was struck by how much smaller the building looked than she remembered. Seeing a line of people inside the door, she hurried in to buy tickets.

Waiting in line, Deena thought about that day when she was in her first-grade classroom at Sam Houston Elementary when the principal interrupted Miss Shelton's lesson on vowels. She remembered his shaky voice over the school's scratchy P.A. system saying President Kennedy had been killed in Dallas. All the children, Deena included, sat in silence, unaware of the magnitude that simple statement carried.

Miss Shelton turned her back to the class for a long while, then took a tissue and stepped into the hall. When her teacher returned and resumed the lesson, Deena found herself staring at the gray metal speaker hanging in the front corner of the room, blaming it for the queasy feeling in her stomach.

Six years later, the entire seventh grade boarded a yellow school bus to Dallas as part of their Texas history study to see the site where Lee Harvey Oswald had assassinated their beloved president. There was no museum, no admittance into the School Book Depository Building, no white 'X' painted outside on Elm Street. That didn't happen until 1989 when the museum opened. But school children across the state stood in Dealey Plaza to honor their slain president, feeling a mixture of awe and resentment.

Stepping off the elevator onto the sixth floor sent chills through Deena. Like many visitors, she and Russell walked past the first few exhibits and headed straight to the glassed-in area along the opposite wall where curators had meticulously recreated the sniper's nest. How odd it felt to see boxes of textbooks piled up—boxes just like the ones Deena received when new books arrived in her classroom. She inched her way through the crowd toward the window just to the right of the sniper's, staring down at the spot on the street that marked where Kennedy was first hit. For a moment, she forgot why she was there. All she could think about was the Kennedys.

She did not need to see the exhibits—detailed displays with enlarged photos of every aspect surrounding that fateful day—because those same images rushed through her head like a movie in fast forward. Jackie in her pink suit, holding roses, greeting the crowd; Jack shaking hands on the tarmac at the airport, pushing his hair off to the side; the Zapruder film—the black car, the crowd waving, the car turning, the shots, the chaos; Walter Cronkite choking back tears, Oswald, Jack Ruby, the riderless horse, the horse-drawn carriage, Jackie's black veil, John John's salute...

"It's all so real," a voice whispered into her ear. She jumped and let out a shrill cry. She turned to see Leon Galt standing right behind her.

"Sorry. Didn't mean to frighten you," he said.

"What are you doing here?" She did not even try to hide her annoyance.

"Are you kidding?" He took a few steps backward and spread out his arms. "This is my home-away-from-home. These are my people. Welcome."

His smile and manner reminded her of a real estate agent showing a house to a prospective buyer.

"Actually," he added, "I was standing near the ticket counter when you walked in. I came up here to say hello."

Russell walked up, recognizing the infamous author. "Are you Noel Future?"

"I am indeed." They shook hands, and it was obvious her brother was star struck.

"I'm Deena's brother, Russell Sinclair. Would you mind autographing these books for me and my buddy?" He reached down into his pocket and pulled out two much-read copies of *Roswell: Inside the Hanger*.

Galt pulled a pen from his shirt pocket as the two men chatted like old friends.

So that's what he was hiding in his shorts. Deena couldn't believe it. She gawked at her brother, hoping he wouldn't ask her to take a picture.

Russell pulled out his cell phone, looked at Deena, and said, "Would you mind taking—" He stopped short when he saw the look on her face. It was a look that said, "Don't you dare!" He put the phone away and took one step back, like a soldier who had just been dressed down by his commanding officer.

"Not as big a fan as your brother, I take it," Galt said to Deena. "I'm signing books down the street until noon. I'll be at Hoffman's around the corner for lunch after that if you'd both care to join me. I know you probably have more questions. Hopefully, I can answer at least a few of them for you."

Deena noticed a change in his demeanor. He was less haughty, more humble.

"Perhaps," she said. "Thanks."

He reached inside his suit coat and pulled out a brochure and handed it to Deena. "Remember, 'X' marks the spot."

She looked down and realized it was a map of the museum and the surrounding grounds, like the one she got with her ticket. "I already have one." She looked up just in time to see Galt walking back through the crowd toward the elevator.

Russell stepped in front of her. "I know you're mad, but I couldn't help it. I mean, it would be like if you met, umm, Harper Lee. You'd be like, 'I love your book. I love Atticus. I love Boo Radley.' Am I right?"

Annoyed that she could never stay mad at her brother, she looked at him and said, "Let the dead bury the dead this time, Mr. Finch."

They went back to the first exhibit and spent the next hour wandering through the detailed displays. A miniature recreation of Dealey Plaza, newspaper articles, short films, photographs, the Warren Report—everything one could imagine related to the assassination. There was even a display about conspiracy theories.

"Look," Russell said, pointing to an article on the wall. "Noel Future wrote this." Deena read silently, not wanting to admit she was somewhat impressed.

"Let's go outside." Russell motioned toward the elevator. "I want to see the grassy knoll."

When they stepped outside into the bright sunlight, Deena reached in her purse for sunglasses. She was not sure which direction to walk, so she got out the map Galt had given her. "This way," she said, and they headed toward Elm Street.

They walked along the sidewalk, watching tourists take turns dodging cars to stand on the 'X' in the road to have their pictures taken. Several people exercised their right to free speech, proclaiming wrongdoings by the government to anyone who would listen...or not. Some people handed out flyers; others had easels and cardboard signs. One man stood on a crate with the words "Soap Box" stenciled on the side.

"Democracy at its finest," Russell said. "Reminds me of the Sixties."

As they walked around, Deena read descriptions from the map. "This is where Abraham Zapruder stood," she said. "Here is where that young couple lay on the grass to protect their children."

They walked up the hill to the fence. "Here is where the second gunman supposedly stood." She looked over the fence into what seemed like an ordinary parking lot filled with ordinary cars. On the broken concrete next to the fence, she saw a faint mark on the ground. "This must be the place," she said, pointing it out to Russell. She looked back at the map and noticed something unusual. The 'X' on the map had been written with an ink pen; it was not pre-printed. 'X' marks the spot, she thought, recalling Galt's words when he gave her the map. She gasped. "Russell! Matthew was the second gunman!"

"And I'm the Easter Bunny," he laughed.

"No, look." She showed him the map, pointing at the ink mark. "Leon Galt thinks Matthew was the second gunman on the grassy knoll!"

"That's insane! That's crazy, and believe me, I *know* crazy."

"What time is it?" she asked, forgetting her brother never wore a watch. She looked down at her own. "Almost 12:30. We need to get to that restaurant before he leaves." They hurried down the street back toward the museum.

The West End, the area of Dallas where they were, had received much-needed revitalization over the past few years. Deena and Gary had been there several times to dine and browse through the high-end boutiques. She knew right where to find the restaurant.

When they went in, the downtown lunch crowd was out in full force. The dimly lit interior, brightened by neon beer signs and television screens, starkly contrasted the solemn memorial they had just left. Tourists and business people alike gathered to soak in the lively, relaxed atmosphere. Texas country, probably Willie, bounced off the high ceiling and exposed brick walls.

Deena's mouth watered as the savory aroma of sizzling steaks and spices blasted her senses. She spotted Galt in a back booth. He smiled as they approached. "I was afraid you weren't going to make it," he said, waving to the waitress as they sat down across from him. "What would you like?"

"Bud Light for me," Russell said. "She'll have iced tea."

"What, no appetite?" Galt was finishing off the last of his steak and baked potato.

Out of breath and exasperated, Deena couldn't seem to form a complete sentence. "The second gunman? The grassy knoll? Really?"

Galt folded his napkin and laid it on the table. "I know it seems hard to believe—"

"Hard to believe?" Russell put both of his hands on the table and leaned in. "It's downright absurd. Now, Mr. Future or Galt or whatever, you know I respect you, I do. But *certainly* you can understand why we would like to hear some proof before you go off publishing such an extreme allegation? I mean, you show up out of the blue asking questions, you mysteriously find my sister, then you tell us you are going to indict our relative in the biggest crime of the twentieth century? You must be able to understand why we are asking for proof."

Deena had never been more proud of her brother than she was at that moment. Whether he was sticking up for her, or Matthew, or their family, she didn't care.

Galt measured his words carefully. "First, let me say that I have sources. Sources who keep me informed."

Deena finally found her voice. "Mark Lancaster? Did he tell you about me?"

"Yes. Your cousin, Mark. See? No big mystery there." The waitress set down their drinks and cleared away Galt's plate. When she left, he continued. "Let me explain how this works," Galt said as if teaching Conspiracy Theory 101.

Russell cupped his hand over his right ear so he could hear over the crowd and music.

"None of us were actually there. You weren't. I wasn't. Therefore, you must construct your theory like you would a tent. Each piece of evidence is a pole. Too few poles, and the tent falls to the ground. Enough poles, and the tent stands sturdy. Even if you lose a pole here or there—maybe one gets a crack—the tent stands up. Your theory stands up. That's about the best you can do."

"So, show me your poles," she said and realized how awkward that sounded. "You know what I mean."

Galt chuckled. "I can only tell you to look at his service record and his associations."

"We know about his army career, about the wet work," Deena said. "But this was some years later. Where's the connection?"

Galt leaned forward. "He may have left the army, but the skills he learned stayed with him. He had a reputation that many people knew about, including people outside our government."

"But an assassin?" Deena's mouth was dry. She took a sip of tea. "He was thirty years old then. Who says he was still a sharpshooter? And, did you know he wore glasses?" Deena thought this piece of information might surprise Galt and put a crack in one of his tent poles.

"Yes. Bifocals. To read. His distance vision was perfect."

Deena was sure her face revealed that she was unaware of that fact.

"Look," Galt said, "you've got to keep an open mind."

Deena argued back. "If what you say is true, why would he do it? Money? Blackmail?"

"Or a combination."

The waitress came by with the check, and Galt handed her his credit card.

"What if he refused?" Deena asked. "Could that be why someone killed him?"

"Sure, but the evidence shows that he didn't refuse."

Russell nodded his head slowly. "And they killed him anyway. Just like Oswald." Russell was drinking Galt's ridiculous Kool-Aid.

Deena protested. "Do you know what will happen if your book comes out and makes this claim?"

"Yes. Matthew Meade and a few others will become household names." Galt thanked the waitress and signed the receipt.

Deena glared across the table. "The press will be all over this. Reporters will stalk our family. The hatred and anger—I can't even imagine."

"And the money." Galt rubbed the tips of his fingers together. "I'll make a fortune, and you all can probably get a piece of the pie as well."

That was the last straw. Where was a stun gun when she need it? She scooted toward Russell, indicating it was time to go. She stood up and looked down defiantly at Galt. "I have a lead, a good lead. If there's a hound dog's chance in Hades that it's true, I'm going to prove it. And when I do, Mr. Galt, your tent is going to come crashing down and take you with it."

And with that, she and Russell marched toward the exit. Perhaps it was just wishful thinking, but she thought she heard him say, "That's what I'm afraid of."

Chapter 26

Deena swerved back and forth onto the highway shoulder as she dug around for something in her purse.

"Watch where you're going! You're going to get us killed," Russell said, gripping the front dash with both hands.

She wanted to talk to Gene Collins again as soon as possible, so she left downtown Dallas and headed straight to Bingham.

"Here it is." She held up the small black address book and handed it to Russell. "We can ask Collins if he knows any of these people. That way we can narrow down who we have to hunt for. Surely someone knows something to back up Henry Wilcox's story. After all this time, we may find someone who will admit to knowing about the warehouse boys and the murder."

Russell flipped through the pages, trying to read the small print. "I don't have my reading glasses, so I can't see a dadgum thing."

"It doesn't really matter because all of the phone numbers are old-style. Each has two letters and four digits. We just need to ask Collins if any of those people worked at Barnes Medical."

Russell stared out at the road. "How long until we get to Bingham? I'm starving and I need to take some medicine."

"We can stop and get a burger. There's a place just a few miles up. It's not Hoffman's, but it'll have to do." Something caught Deena's eye in the rearview mirror. "Crap-a-doodle-doo!"

A highway patrol car, lights flashing, pulled in behind her.

"Be cool." Russell said, as she pulled onto the shoulder to stop.

"Why wouldn't I be cool? I haven't committed a crime or anything." She waited while the officer got out of his car and approached her window.

"Hello, officer." She heard Russell grumble something unintelligible. Ignoring him, she asked, "How are you today?"

The officer leaned down a little to see inside the car, making eye contact with a nervous Russell. "Ma'am, I need to see your license and registration."

"Yes, sir." She got her wallet and started to hand it to him.

"Take it out, please." She obeyed, and then reached over in front of Russell to unlatch the glove compartment. Feeling around for the packet of papers that Gary always made sure was up to date, her hand touched something solid and metal. She leaned over closer to see a gun in her glove compartment. A low gasp escaped from Russell's mouth. Be cool, she thought, and reached under it for the plastic folder. "Here you go, officer," she said in a forced, pleasant voice.

He took the paper, examined it, and walked back to his police cruiser.

"What the—?"

"It's mine," Russell whispered. He quickly closed the glove box. "I put it in your car when we drove up to see Henry Wilcox. I forgot all about it."

"Is it legal? Will we get in trouble if he sees it? Oh, here he comes." They both sat up straight, unnaturally so.

"Ma'am, have you been drinking today?"

"Drinking? Only iced tea, sir."

"I observed you weaving back and forth a few miles back. Can you explain?"

"Why yes, officer. I was trying to find something in my purse, and I guess I was being careless. My brother," she said, motioning to Russell, "told me to be more careful."

He looked back and forth at the two of them. "Would you mind getting out of the car? Both of you."

This is it. We are both going to jail.

"You can just stand right there," he said, pointing to Russell. "Ma'am, if you'd come over here, I need you to perform a few tests."

Like an obedient child, Deena followed.

"Watch me as I demonstrate." The highway patrolman spread his arms out and touched his nose using one hand at a time.

If I weren't about to go to jail, this would be funny, Deena thought. She performed the task flawlessly. He then had her walk a straight line. Luckily, she was wearing sandals and not heels.

"Thank you. You can both return to your vehicle and wait for me." He went back to his car and stood there writing on a large notepad.

"What do you think?" she asked Russell as she sat staring out the front window. "Are we going to be okay?"

"Maybe." They waited for what seemed a lifetime until the officer returned.

"Ma'am, I am issuing you a citation for reckless driving. I need you to sign it to indicate you received the citation. It does not mean you agree. There is information on the back about what you will need to do."

"Thank you," she said, signing and taking her copy.

"I suggest you be more careful and pay attention to the road. Have a nice day."

"Thank you, I will." She pressed the button to roll up her window and let out a huge sigh of relief. After waiting for an opening in the traffic, she carefully drove off.

"Take the next exit," Russell ordered. "There's a Dairy Queen. I'll put the pistol in the cargo bin."

Walking inside to order their meal, Deena realized she was still shaking. After they settled in the booth to eat, she finally asked her brother the million-dollar question. "Why did you bring a gun? I thought you said you didn't have any bullets."

"I don't. It's not loaded. I just didn't know what we'd be up against with Henry Wilcox, and I wanted to be prepared."

She waited for a young mother with her daughter to walk past, and then asked, "How is an unloaded gun going to help? Are you going to throw it at somebody or what?"

"I know, I know. You're not a gun person, so you wouldn't understand."

"I could just see us now. 'Hey Mister Criminal, give us a minute to run to the sporting goods store to buy some ammo, and we'll be right back.'"

Russell ate his sandwich without speaking. After a few minutes, he said, "Let's focus on the matter at hand—Gene Collins."

"I want you to go in with me. Maybe he'll be more intimidated if we're both there." She wiped salt off her blouse from the French fries she was eating. "There's a lot riding on this meeting. If Collins doesn't admit to Wilcox's theory, Matthew could go from sympathetic victim to notorious killer."

"MR. COLLINS, YOU HAVE visitors," the attendant announced. Deena stepped into the doorway with her brother right behind.

"You again?" he asked. "What do you want now?"

"Mr. Collins, this is my brother Russell, and we need to ask you a few more questions."

"Good thing you came today. I might not be here tomorrow, if you know what I mean." He picked up the remote and muted the television. "I'm not really in the mood to answer questions, but being that you're Matthew's kin and all, fire away."

They sat down at the table across from him and Deena took the lead. "I'm not exactly sure how to ask this, but here goes. Do you know anything about people stealing merchandise at Barnes Medical while you were there?" She watched his reaction closely.

The old man leaned back in his chair. "Obviously you know something or you wouldn't be asking about it."

"The information I received is that you and others working in the warehouse had a scam going where you were taking inventory and selling it on the black market. I was also told that you all were caught and fired. Is that true?"

"Which part?"

"All of it."

"Yes and no," Collins said. "Yeah, merchandise would walk out the back door, but we're not talking about some big organized crime here. Just a little employee pilfering now and then. Why do you ask? What does this have to do with Matthew?"

"So, were you fired?"

"First, tell me the connection."

"My source," Deena said, staring him right in the eyes, "accused you and your partners of killing my uncle."

"That's not true! Matthew Meade was my best friend. I would never do anything like that, not to him or anyone." He choked and took a swig of water.

Russell took a softer tone. "I know how it is, man. Fighting in the war does things to you. You are taught to kill over there, and when you come back here...you know."

"No, I don't. I'm telling the truth." Collins coughed. "Look, I don't know who you talked to, but this is the truth. A couple of us were helping ourselves to some of the merchandise and selling it on the side. Someone ratted on us to Matthew. He said for us to cut it out, or he'd have to tell management. I told him I would stop, and I told my buddies to do the same. One of them kept it up. A few weeks later, we all got canned. The boss didn't know who to trust, so we all went down for it."

Deena, noticing Gene appeared more haggard than on her first visit, could see he was visibly shaken.

He pushed himself up from the table and leaned on his cane as he walked toward the night table. He opened the drawer and took out a bottle of medicine. When he came back to the table, he washed down a pill with a gulp of water.

"At my age," he said. "I have no reason to lie."

Deena looked at him for a minute, trying to decide if she believed him. Then she asked, "What about that last night at the diner? You said you left the table to go to the men's room. Is that true?"

He looked down and shook his head. "I don't know who you talked to, but it feels like I'm being haunted by a ghost. No, it's not true. I went to use the pay phone. I called this girl I was seeing, Katherine Cooper. You showed me her picture, remember? She used to be engaged to Matthew, but he broke it off. I know I shouldn't have taken up with my best friend's ex-girlfriend, but I couldn't help it. When the cops asked me about that night at the diner, I lied. For all I knew, Matthew was going to turn up a few days later. I didn't want him to find out I was seeing his girl."

It was a plausible explanation. "What happened to her?"

"When I got fired, she dropped me. I moved back here to Bingham." His eyes were moist from age and regret.

"Is there a chance anyone at the warehouse would have had a grudge against Matthew?" Deena asked.

"No way. Everyone liked him. We trusted him."

Reaching into her purse, Deena pulled out the address book. "Can you look through here and tell me if any of these people worked with you?"

He squinted and handed it back. "This writing is too small. Read it out."

As she called out the names, she marked the ones Collins recognized from the company. He noted that two of the employees had passed away, leaving five others.

Deena focused on one name. "I'd really like to track down Donna Morrison. Would any of these other people have kept up with her?"

"I don't know, but you should call Carolyn Fitzhugh. If anyone will know what happened to her, Carolyn will. She's into everybody's business in Maycroft. Have you heard of her?"

"I know who she is, but I have never met her."

"She goes to the Baptist church. Used to be a big community do-gooder."

Deena knew about the family's reputation. "There's a Fitzhugh Park, Fitzhugh Library, Fitzhugh Women's Shelter."

"That's her," Gene said. "She's slowed down the last few years. Has heart trouble, like me."

"Thanks. I'll call her."

"Sis," Russell said. "Would you mind giving Gene and me a minute alone?"

She was surprised but trusted her brother. "Okay, sure. Mr. Collins, I appreciate your help once again. I hope you feel better."

He nodded to her as she stood up and walked out into the hall. Standing right next to the door, she listened as her brother began to speak.

"Gene, if what you say is true, then someone else murdered Matthew. This may sound like a strange question, but did Matthew ever say he was approached by someone wanting to hire him for some private work? Like a hit?"

Deena leaned even closer to the doorway and heard Collins respond. "How do you know about that?"

Russell stood up, walked over to the door, and pushed it until the latch clicked.

DEENA SAT IN HER CAR fidgeting while waiting for Russell. After about ten minutes, she couldn't wait any longer. Locking her door, she headed toward the entrance.

Right then, Russell barreled around the corner. "Let's get out of here."

Annoyed with her brother, Deena stood waiting with her hands on her hips. "What happened? What did he say?"

"I'll drive." He held out his hand, waiting for Deena to give him the keys.

Frustrated that he was not answering her questions, she handed them over and got in the passenger seat.

They both jumped as an ambulance drove past them, sirens blaring, pulling into the back parking lot of the building.

Russell backed out, almost hitting another car.

"Be careful," she said. "You don't want to get us killed."

He glanced at her. "Poor choice of words."

"What do you mean?"

"Gene Collins. I think he's dead."

Deena gasped. "You killed him?"

"No, of course not! He had a heart attack. He was talking and suddenly grabbed his chest and keeled over. I got a nurse and they kicked me out of the room."

"So that ambulance..."

"Yeah. Poor guy. I hope he makes it."

They drove in silence a few minutes, and Russell turned toward the highway. "You are not going to believe this," he said, looking in his rearview mirror.

"What? What did he say?"

"No. You're not going to believe who is following us. Leon Galt."

Deena turned around to look. "What the blazes does he want now?"

Galt flashed his lights at them.

"He wants us to pull over." Russell glanced at his sister. "What do you want to do?"

"I don't want to talk to him until you tell me what Collins said."

"Okay then. If I speed up, maybe he'll get the message we are not in the mood to talk." Russell pulled into the left lane to pass several large trucks.

"Be careful," Deena said. "There's some road construction up here."

"He's speeding up. This guy is a slow learner." Russell pulled back into the right lane to pass a slower car. Galt was on his tail. "I've got an idea. I'm going to slow down, pull onto the shoulder, and he'll go flying by."

Deena braced herself. Russell put on the brakes, pulled off onto the shoulder, and came to a stop. Just as planned, they watched Galt's black sedan speed past.

Impressed, Deena asked, "Where'd you learn that move? The army?"

"No, *Top Gun*."

They saw Galt's brake lights come on as he pulled onto the gravel shoulder. But, instead of stopping, his car fishtailed then flew off the road into the grassy embankment, flipping over once before landing upright. Steam immediately began pouring out from under the hood.

"Whoa!" Russell said as he drove slowly down the shoulder toward the scene.

Other cars pulled off the road, and a man raced toward the wreck shouting to his friends, "Call 9-1-1!" Several people had their cell phones out and stood back watching. Deena and Russell got out just as they saw Galt open the door and emerge from his car. He pulled out his handkerchief and blotted it on his forehead, checking for blood. A few drops trickled from a small cut.

"Dude! Are you okay?" the young man asked, giving Galt a shoulder to lean on. "You could have been killed!"

"Yeah. I think I'm alright."

The guy shook his head. "Your car is toast."

Seeing Russell and Deena coming to help, he left Galt standing with them and headed toward the car along with some other curious onlookers.

"Leon, are you okay? Do you need to sit down?" Deena felt guilty and helpless.

"*Top Gun*, right?" Galt asked.

"I'm sorry, man," Russell said. "I didn't mean for you to—"

"Not your fault. I shouldn't have followed you. I tried to catch you when you left the nursing home, but you took off too fast." He put his hand up on his shoulder and rubbed it. "I just needed to talk to you in person."

Sirens announced the arrival of several emergency vehicles. "I have a proposition for you." He swayed a little, and Russell caught him by the arm.

"I think that's going to have to wait," Russell said.

Paramedics rushed down the hill as Russell helped Galt to the ground.

"Are you two hurt?" one of the paramedics asked.

"No. We weren't in the car," Deena said. "We just—saw what happened." She and Russell backed out of the way and watched as Galt answered their questions.

"You have my number," Deena said, and she and Russell walked up the hill to their car.

Police officers were talking to other witnesses. She took the keys and got in the driver's seat. "I've talked to the police once today. That's enough." Inching her way around a fire engine, she pulled into the backed-up, single lane of traffic and drove toward Crossbow.

"Are you going to tell Gary about this?"

"Of course. But first things first. What did Gene tell you?"

Russell took a deep breath as the accident scene grew smaller in his side mirror. "I guess you heard what I asked him. Apparently, about six months before he disappeared, someone approached Matthew to do a job. Offered to compensate him really well for his work. He refused but told Collins about it because he wanted someone to watch his back."

"Did Matthew say who it was or what the job was?" She glanced nervously from the road to her brother.

"No. He said Matthew never mentioned it again."

"If the guy was looking for a hired gun, he doesn't sound very persistent."

"I agree. You would think he would have ways of convincing Matthew."

"Did you ask Collins if he ever told the police about it?"

"Yes, but that's when he...stopped talking."

"I see. Well, I'm going to call Carolyn Fitzhugh first thing tomorrow to see if she knows where we can find Donna. The fact that she was there and moved away a week later seems pretty suspicious to me."

They drove in silence for a while, thinking about all that had just happened.

When they were almost to Russell's, he shifted in his seat to look straight at his sister. "Deena, why are you doing this? Does it really matter at this point? Is it about the job at the newspaper?"

She thought about it. When she pulled in front of his house, she could hear Maggie barking in the distance. Leaning back in her seat, she let out a deep sigh. "You know, that's a good question. At first, it seemed exciting. I might write an interesting story and get a job while also helping Gran get some closure. Then, it became bigger. More of a matter of right versus wrong."

Russell nodded. "With Galt being the one wrongfully accusing Matthew of murder."

"Now," she said, "it's more about finding the truth of what really did or did not happen."

"Are you saying that if Galt's evidence proves Matthew's involvement in the assassination, you will just sit back and let the chips fall where they may?"

"What choice do we have? And besides, isn't finding the truth the most important thing?"

"I'm not so sure," Russell said. "Sometimes, the truth hurts more than it helps."

"I'm beginning to see that." Motioning toward the back of the car, she said, "Don't forget to take that thing with you."

"Will do."

Deena watched as Russell took the gun and walked to his front door. Opening it, he leaned down to scratch the dog and took the gun straight to the safe—where he had previously left the door ajar when he first took it out.

As she pulled her car back around to head toward home, she repeated her brother's words in her head. *Sometimes the truth hurts more than it helps.*

Chapter 27

L eon Galt lay in his hospital bed, aching from head to toe. "No," he repeated into the phone. "Let it go. And by the way, there won't be any more money coming your way." He ended the call and laid his cell phone next to him on the hospital bed.

A nurse walked in with a plate of cookies. "Someone brought you a treat, Mr. Galt." She set the plate on the side table and moved his pillow back into place. "Do you need anything while I'm here?"

"Stronger pain killers."

She smiled, saying, "I'll see what I can do."

He reached for the note and read the name: Deena Sharpe. He threw it down. *I wouldn't be surprised if they were laced with arsenic.*

Chapter 28

Gary made Deena promise to stay out of trouble when he left for work on Monday, waving the ticket she had received like a declaration of war. Although he was as concerned as she was about the outlook of Matthew's legacy, he cared more about his wife's safety than her obsession with finding answers. Apparently getting a ticket for reckless driving, causing a man to have a heart attack, and sending another man careening off the road were a little too much excitement for him to ignore.

Consequently, she didn't tell him that she drove back to Bingham on Sunday with a plate of store-bought cookies for Leon Galt. She told him they were for a "sick friend," which was not exactly a lie. He *was* in the hospital, and she *had* seen him more often than her other friends lately.

When the nurse had told Deena he was in surgery for a broken hand, she left the plate with a post-it note that read, *Get well soon. -Deena.*

It was the least she could do since they'd almost killed him.

Carolyn Fitzhugh was not in the phone book, but that didn't stop Deena. She had a hunch Sandra would know how to get in touch with her. All the bigwigs in town supported the animal shelter and Sandra's thrift store. Besides, she wanted to go to the shop for a new umbrella since the weatherman was finally predicting rain.

Sandra closed the store on Mondays during the winter months, but it was deep into tourist season and she needed all the business she could get. She looked up from the register when the bells on the door jingled. "Welcome." She smiled at Deena, continuing to help her customer.

The glass and pottery aisle, as always, called Deena's name, and she answered by making a beeline to its jam-packed shelves. Several new pieces of pottery peeked out from behind a set of blue-rimmed margarita glasses. She carefully picked them up, admiring their colorful Southwestern designs. They were perfect to sell at her booth, so she took them both up to the counter.

She walked over to the purses and accessories. A vintage parasol stuck out of the umbrella stand next to the scarves and gloves. She picked it up and saw that most of the silk was tattered, too worn out for her to purchase. Several folding umbrellas lay in a bin, including a red one with white polka dots.

When she opened it, Sandra's voice screeched from across the store. "Not inside! It's bad luck!"

Deena quickly closed the umbrella, feeling like a teenager caught making out with her boyfriend. She had forgotten how superstitious her friend was and waited for the customer at the counter to leave before walking up to the register. "Sorry," she said, "but I don't think it's possible to have any worse luck than I've had lately."

"Knock on wood," Sandra ordered, and they both tapped their knuckles on the oak countertop. "Are you talking about your uncle's case?"

"Yep. And by the way, that picture I showed you was indeed an engagement photo."

"I thought so," Sandra said with a self-congratulatory grin. "Anytime you want me to be your assistant sleuth, just say the word."

She rang up the two vases and then picked up the umbrella. "This is in good working condition," she said. "I test all the umbrellas I get before I put them on the shelf. Outside, of course. This one is on the house since I scared the bejeebers out of you."

"Thanks," Deena laughed and pulled out her credit card to pay for the pottery. She heard something shuffle behind the counter and peered around the corner. "Who's this?" she asked when she spotted a black ball of fluff.

"This is Pepper." Sandra untied the leash from her stool and walked the shy little puppy around to Deena who bent down to pet the little dog. "We are trying to socialize her, so I thought she might spend the day at the shop. She was found in a dumpster about two weeks ago. Isn't she adorable?"

Deena felt a tug at her heart as she rubbed the neck and ears of the precious pooch. "I can't believe no one has adopted her."

"Oh, that won't be a problem. She's just too young still. There's even a waiting list for her. It's the older, not-so-pretty ones that we have trouble re-homing." She reached into a small bag and pulled out a treat for the pup. "It reminds me of the treasures I sell in this shop. You see a sweet, flawless Hummel figurine, and it flies off the shelf. Then you have another one with a chip on the girl's bow or maybe the boy's arm has been glued back on, and you can't give it away."

Deena shook her head, knowing she was guilty of seeing things that way.

"Things don't have to be perfect to have value," Sandra said.

"You're right. If it were the same with people, we'd all be living in dumpsters."

Sandra laughed. "When you finally decide to get a dog, let me know. I'll help you pick one out." She winked at her friend.

Deena snapped her fingers. "I almost forgot the reason I came in today. Do you know Carolyn Fitzhugh?"

"Of course. Doesn't everyone? Oh, I forget you aren't originally from Maycroft. She's quite a character."

"I was hoping to get a chance to talk to her about someone I am trying to locate."

"Her daughter, Estelle, takes care of her now. I could call to see if she is up for a visit. Keep an eye on things and I'll be right back." Sandra disappeared into the storeroom as several new customers milled around the shop.

Deena spied them suspiciously, hoping they wouldn't try to shoplift. She didn't want to bust some heads. Working on her uncle's murder case had been empowering, and she was feeling more of her inner Lara Croft lately.

Sandra returned within a few minutes. "You are expected at the residence of Mrs. Carolyn Fitzhugh at precisely two o'clock this afternoon. I hope that's okay," Sandra said and wrote the address on a notepad.

"Perfect. Thanks, Watson."

"If you want to win her over, I suggest two things: Wear a dress and take a gift."

Deena's face twisted in displeasure. "I can handle the dress part—if I have to—but what sort of gift should I take?"

"I bet she would just *love* a pretty Southwestern vase," Sandra said, handing the shopping bag to Deena. "Oh, and whatever you do, don't mention her brother."

Chapter 29

As she pulled into the long driveway that led to the Fitzhugh house, Deena wondered if her navy and white dress was fancy enough for her visit to "Lady Fitzhugh." She lived in one of the large houses on the outskirts of town that most people only drive by when showing visitors historic landmarks.

Often referred to as the "Grande Dame of Maycroft," Carolyn lost her husband nearly twenty years earlier but kept her social standing and estate in perfect order.

Deena, gift in hand, lifted the gothic brass knocker on the front door and waited for her hostess. A housekeeper wearing a uniform and little hat opened the door and escorted Deena to the parlor. An impressive staircase wound its way down and emptied into the large foyer. She glanced around the eclectic décor. A large urn with a bird-like figure balanced on a marble column. A western cowboy scene hung on the opposite wall.

The housekeeper deposited Deena in the parlor, motioning for her to sit on a red velvet sofa.

The built-in shelves across from her were filled with assorted knick knacks, everything from a brightly painted totem pole to a large ivory elephant. It looked like Jane Austen meets Annie Oakley.

The doors opened wide, and Estelle pushed her mother's wheelchair into the room and parked her across from Deena.

"Hello Mrs. Fitzhugh. I'm Deena Sharpe."

Looking her over, the woman said, "How do you do, my dear. This is my daughter, Estelle."

Poor Estelle seemed out of breath, most likely from helping her mother get ready for the visit. She was about Deena's age, but seemed older. She nodded and sat in a straight-back chair at the end of the rosewood coffee table.

"You have a lovely home," Deena said politely. "Thank you for seeing me on such short notice. I brought you a small gift."

"My, what a sweet gesture." Mrs. Fitzhugh opened the package and admired the piece of pottery. "Such a pretty vase," she said and handed it to Estelle who carried it out of the room. "Would you care for some tea?"

A glass of iced tea sounded perfect. "I'd love some."

Mrs. Fitzhugh pulled out a small silver bell that was hiding somewhere under the layers of fabric beneath her crocheted shawl. The maid returned promptly with a full silver tea service.

Hot tea? In the middle of July?

"I'll mind it." The housekeeper left the room just as Estelle tip-toed back in and took her seat. Mrs. Fitzhugh proceeded to go through the ritual of tea service, from cream to lemon to sugar cubes. She seemed to be enjoying herself. When she finally finished, she picked up her cup and blew on it. "You taught at the high school, is that right?"

"Yes," Deena said, surprised by the comment.

"Too bad you lost your job. That poor Haskett girl. Such a shame."

Deena was at a loss for words. She sat holding her teacup mid-air, steam opening the pores on her face.

"And your husband is a financial advisor. Such a handsome man. Reminds me of Jonathan Baker who used to raise horses down the road."

Deena offered a weak smile. This old busy-body had more information than the FBI.

"Now, what can I do for you, dear?" Mrs. Fitzhugh held her cup and saucer and tilted her head like a queen granting an audience to one of her lowly subjects.

"Well," Deena said, still feeling caught off guard, "I wanted to see if you know a woman I am looking for."

Her hostess smiled, saying, "I know everyone, dear." Then she placed the dainty china cup to her lips.

"This woman hasn't lived in Maycroft for years."

"As I said, I know everyone." She took a sip.

"Then I guess you know Donna Morrison."

With that, Earl Grey spewed from the old woman's mouth, spraying a shower of hot tea all over her and the table.

"Mother!" Estelle cried. She grabbed the tea towels and began wildly blotting the doilies around her mother's neck and chest.

"Stop that! Stop!" Mrs. Fitzhugh yelled, slapping away her daughter's hands as if swatting flies.

Deena calmly took a drink from her cup to hide her uncontrollable grin, hoping the wicked witch didn't melt.

"I'm afraid you will have to leave," Estelle said. Deena put down her cup and stood.

"No! Sit!" Mrs. Fitzhugh ordered. Deena sat, awaiting her next command.

"Stop that!" she yelled again at Estelle who had moved on to wiping up the tray and table. "Remove this tray!" Estelle began to pick it up. "Not you, Irene!" She rang the bell furiously, and the housekeeper rushed in. "Take this tray and take her with you!" Estelle and Irene left the parlor and closed the doors behind them.

Mrs. Fitzhugh took several deep breaths to regain her composure. Her jaw was set as she looked sternly at Deena. "How do you know Donna Morrison?"

"I don't. I just know who she is. I'm trying to locate her."

"Why? What on earth would you want from that harlot?" She wrung her hands in her lap.

"I am looking into the death of my uncle."

"Matthew Meade," she said.

"Yes. Did you know him?"

Mrs. Fitzhugh gave Deena a stern look and did not answer.

"Donna Morrison was with Matthew on the night he disappeared. I would like to talk to her to see if she can offer any insight as to what was happening with Matthew and the company where they both worked." Deena shifted in her chair, waiting for Mrs. Fitzhugh to respond.

In measured words, she finally said, "Donna Morrison is what we used to call a 'floozy.' She was a gold digger looking for a sugar daddy. She found one in my brother."

Deena cringed, remembering the warning she had gotten from Sandra.

"Glenn had big plans, political aspirations, but he put all that in jeopardy when he took up with that woman. He was married, you see, and had a son. He would sneak around to see her while his poor wife took care of the house and that baby." Her eyes began to glisten; she was caught up in her memories.

"Something eventually got to him. Maybe it was guilt...maybe it was just the liquor. He started drinking heavily and was fired. That was the end of his political career. They moved to Houston to be near his wife's family, but it only got worse. The best thing that ever happened to him was when he drove off a ravine one night and was killed."

How could anyone be so cold-hearted about their own child? Deena asked, "Did his wife know about the affair?"

"Of course. Women can sense these things, you know. But she stayed with him. After he died, she married herself a real nice fellow and had two more children."

Afraid to get too personal, Deena decided to ask anyway. "Do you blame your brother or Donna for his downfall?"

Mrs. Fitzhugh hesitated. "Both."

They sat in awkward silence for a long moment. Deena was not sure what to do or say.

Mrs. Fitzhugh spoke up first. "I understand why you would want to talk to her. I'll give you the information I have." She picked up the bell and rang it again. When Estelle opened the door tentatively, Mrs. Fitzhugh ordered, "Get me my book."

Deena picked up her purse and fumbled around for pen and paper.

Estelle returned with a thick, black leather-bound book. She handed it to her mother and walked over to stand by one of the room's heavily draped windows.

At first, Deena thought Estelle had brought in the family bible. In a way, though, it was. The book contained Mrs.

Fitzhugh's years of contacts, each entry neatly written in her own handwriting.

"Here is the latest information I have. Her married name is McCaig. Must have married an Irishman." She wrinkled her nose as if smelling something foul. "What did you say your name was again?" She looked at her guest suspiciously.

"Deena Sharpe."

"Sharpe. Oh yes, a good English name," she said and relaxed. "Her address is 1289 Riley Road in Fort Worth. That should help you locate her."

"Thank you so much, Mrs. Fitzhugh." Deena picked up her purse and stood.

"I enjoyed your visit very much, Mrs. Sharpe. You are welcome to return any time."

Deena nodded and, for some unknown reason, performed a half curtsy and followed Estelle to the door.

Once on the front porch, Estelle lowered her voice to a whisper. "Be careful when you talk to Donna Morrison. Mother once told me she tried to blackmail my Uncle Glenn. She might try to get money out of you, too."

Deena nodded and then hurried down the paved pathway. More secrets, she thought. Everyone had them.

PARKING IN FRONT OF the Fitzhugh Public Library, Deena noted the irony. She hoped to find a current Fort Worth telephone directory. The girl at the counter was a former student, another one whose name Deena could not remember.

"Hi, Mrs. Sharpe. How's it going?"

Deena used her fallback greeting. "Hey *you*!" The extra dash of enthusiasm always helped. "I'm good. How have *you* been?"

"I'm going back to UT in the fall."

"That's great. So, I was wondering if you all would have a copy of the Fort Worth phone directory."

"Sure, we have it online. I'll show you."

They walked over to the small computer station and the girl got Deena started.

"McCaig," Deena said as she typed the name into the search bar. She looked for a listing on Riley Road. Bingo! There it was. Michael McCaig. She wrote down the phone number and closed the program. As she walked back toward the counter, her eyes were drawn like magnets to the fiction section. Then she pictured the stack of mysteries on her night table that she had put off reading and decided against perusing the shelves. Before she knew it, she bumped into a tall pedestal, nearly knocking a marble bust to the floor. She grabbed it and set it upright, carefully stepping back to make sure it was steady. The gold nameplate screamed at her to be more careful. It read: Carolyn R. Fitzhugh. *Great. Now she's stalking me.*

She passed the counter on her way out. "Thank *you*. Good to see *you*." Chiding herself, she thought, the older I get, the more students I have named "You."

Anxious to call Donna, she sat in the car and used her cell phone to dial the number. Two rings, three, four...

"Hello," a woman said.

Suddenly, Deena realized she had not thought about what she would say. She would have to wing it. "Is this Donna Morrison? I mean McCaig?"

"Yes, to both," the woman said. "Who is this? If you're selling something, I'm not buying."

"No, no. My name is Deena Sharpe. Matthew Meade was my uncle." She waited, hoping the other woman would speak first. She didn't. "Did you used to work at Barnes Medical Supply?"

"Yes."

"Did you know Matthew Meade?"

"Yes."

"Did you know that his body was identified a few months ago?"

"Yes, I read about it in the paper. I suppose you want to ask me about the night he disappeared."

"Yes." Deena held her breath and crossed her toes. She didn't want to have to beg.

Donna hesitated. "You say he was your uncle?"

"That's right. Now that we know he was murdered, I am trying to find out everything I can about his disappearance."

"I told the cops, investigators, everybody who asked me, what happened that night." Donna paused again. "I'll make you a deal. You can have one hour and ask me all the questions you want. But after that, I never want to hear from you again."

Deena's pulse raced. "That sounds fair. You name the time and place."

"It needs to be in public." Donna thought a moment and then said, "How about tomorrow night. There's a place in the Stockyards called Jerry's. I'll be there with my husband at nine o'clock."

"Perfect," Deena said, scribbling down the details.

"I'm only doing this for one reason. You're his kin, and kin means a lot to me." She hung up.

Donna did not sound like the cheating blackmailer Mrs. Fitzhugh had described. Obviously, a lot can change in fifty years. Maybe Donna could help fill in some of the pieces of this puzzle before it was too late.

A strong wind blew dark clouds across the sky. Large drops of water turned to mud on the windshield. The temperature dropped. Searing heat became suffocating humidity.

Deena pulled into the garage just as the sprinkle turned into a shower. Her cell phone rang inside her purse, but she let it go as she hurried into the house. Although they were desperate for rain, this was the kind of storm that brings with it a foreboding feeling. Deena shivered even though she was far from cold.

After setting her purse on the kitchen counter, she pulled out her phone and looked at the number for the missed call. She expected it to be Gary, but it was an unfamiliar number. The caller left a voice message. It was Leon Galt. He wanted her to come to the hospital to discuss an important matter, saying it had to be now or never.

Chapter 30

As soon as **Gary** entered the house, Deena accosted him. "We've got to go."

"What? Where?"

Deena grabbed her bag and headed to the door. "To the hospital to talk to Leon Galt."

"Now? What about dinner?"

"We can eat afterward. Please?"

Gary trailed after her and got in the car. "What's so important this time?"

"He says he has a proposition for us. He is being discharged tomorrow morning, so it has to be today."

Gary turned on the wipers and the defroster to clear the fog from his windshield. "Frankly, I am ready for this whole thing to be over. You are no closer to having an answer than you were a month ago. I'm ready to use a big hammer on this guy, legally speaking, and be done with him."

"I totally agree. No more playing games. He either tells us what he knows or we call his publisher and threaten a lawsuit. Even if we can't disprove what he says, no publisher wants to be sued."

They drove to the Bingham County Hospital, just on the outskirts of Bingham. Deena talked about her visits to the thrift store and to Mrs. Fitzhugh. Gary was jealous that she got a look at the inside of the legendary house. She told him about her scheduled meeting with Donna Morrison.

"Tomorrow? I have out-of-town clients coming in tomorrow. Jeff and I have to take them to dinner. In fact, I was hoping you would go."

"I'm sorry, but I really don't want to push it by calling her back."

"No, you probably shouldn't. I am not letting you go by yourself, though. Either Russell goes with you, or I'll make an excuse to Jeff."

"I'm sure Russell can go." She knew what her husband was thinking even before he said it. "Don't worry. We'll be good."

"There's supposed to be more rain tomorrow night. I don't want you driving back that late in a storm. Promise me you'll get a hotel room in Fort Worth and come home in the morning."

"But that—"

"Promise," Gary said.

"Okay."

When they pulled up to the hospital, Deena opened her new umbrella and they walked quickly to the front door.

"Follow me," she said, leading the way to the elevator and then the room. The door was propped open.

Leon Galt was fully dressed and seated in a chair across from the hospital bed. "Please sit down," he said, motioning to a green vinyl sofa.

Deena looked around and noticed the untouched plate she had brought on Sunday.

Galt followed her eyes. "Can I offer you anything?" he asked. "Water or maybe a...cookie?"

Gary started to speak, and Deena smacked his foot with hers.

"No thanks," Gary said.

"No doubt you are anxious to hear what I have to offer. I'm ready to lay all my cards on the table. No more games."

"That would be refreshing," Deena said. She sat back and crossed her arms.

He had a notepad in his lap and began rifling through the pages, keeping his bandaged hand slightly elevated. "Matthew Meade was a top marksman in the army. He served under MacArthur and then Ridgeway in Korea. He performed special assignments. After he was discharged, his reputation followed him. He was one of three men considered to be the best shooters the military had ever seen. One of the men died in a house fire in 1960. That left your uncle and another man who had moved to Brazil in 1961.

"When a certain foreign group with communist ties decided to eliminate the president, they were led to people familiar with Oswald. He was a loose cannon, though, and they didn't trust him to get the job done. I have several telegrams exchanged between two operatives arranging for a shooter. Both mention MSM, your uncle. I have an affidavit signed by one of these men stating he met with your uncle in May of 1963 offering him a deal. Meade refused to cooperate, which they found unacceptable." Galt paused and asked, "Do you have any questions so far?"

"I assume you have these documents if we needed to see them," Deena said.

"Of course. Now, I admit, the next part is a little speculative. According to my source, they continued to apply pressure to Meade. They threatened to harm his parents. Apparently, he gave in."

"Apparently?" Gary asked.

"That's when my source says he was pulled to work on another job. However, if you compare the description of your uncle to eyewitness reports of the man behind the fence on the grassy knoll, they're a good match. Obviously, they wouldn't keep him around after that, so they shot him and dumped his body on that old farm."

Deena's nose itched, a sure sign she was not convinced. "What do you think happened between the time he disappeared and November 22?"

"They would have kept him in a safe location, working out the details of the plan."

Deena and Gary sat in silence, processing the information.

"I have a question," Deena said at last. "If Matthew was such a good shot, why wasn't Kennedy hit from the front or side?"

"Again, this is speculation. I think he realized that Oswald had done the job and shot high. Either that or he lost his nerve and missed on purpose. Both scenarios, however, explain why witnesses heard more shots than were found to have hit the president."

"This foreign group you mentioned, are you going to tell us who that is?" Deena asked.

"No. If the book isn't released, I need to keep that information concealed for now—for safety reasons."

"Aunt Lucy said you asked her about people with Russian names."

"One name actually, *Zoyenka*. It was a code word. You might find it mentioned in your uncle's papers. It would prove they made contact with him. I don't suppose you have seen it anywhere?"

"No," Deena said. "In your book, did you call him a willing participant or what?"

"I describe his role just as I told it to you. I even call it speculation."

Deena and Gary eyed each other. "What do you think?" Gary asked.

"To be honest," she said, "it sounds reasonable but thin."

Fumbling with the pad of paper, Galt pulled out a typed document and handed it to Gary. "I am hoping this offer will close some of the holes you see in the story. I am offering you ten thousand dollars to spend in any way you like if you get Cora Meade to sign this release form, waiving all rights to legal action in connection with this book."

"You're kidding!" Deena exclaimed. "You are bribing us?"

"Not a bribe—a fee for services rendered. I can have a check cut as soon as you get me a notarized signature. As far as the money goes, you can keep it, give it to charity, or give your grandmother a really nice funeral— someday, that is."

Boiling inside, Deena tried to remain calm. "Mr. Galt, I'm afraid you have misjudged us. We have no intention of making money off the death of my uncle."

"Are you sure?" Galt asked. "You were willing to use the story to land a job. That's not much different. And your cousin, Mark, he seemed more than willing to take advantage of my generosity and help me out."

"Mark took money?" She figured he was involved but would never have believed he was actually working for Galt.

"How do you think I got your cell phone number and always seemed to know where you were? He has been very helpful." Looking at Gary as though they were pals, Galt said, "Perhaps you two should think this over. Talk to your family and see what they say. I'm flying out on Wednesday. My cell number is on that document. Call me as soon as you have a decision."

Gary stood up, towering over Galt. "What if we tell you we intend to sue you and your publisher if this book is released? What do you say to that?"

"Unless you have contradictory evidence, I say that's just more publicity—more sales—more money. I know it sounds crass, but in my line of work, that's just how it is."

Deena got up and stood by her husband. "Don't worry," she said. "You will definitely be hearing from us again."

They walked out of the room and got on the elevator.

Gary did not even bother to crouch under the umbrella as they hurried through the rain to the car. When they settled inside, he turned to Deena. "Look, I know this is important to you, but it has to end. Go meet with that woman tomorrow night, but that's it. You know I support you, but I'm worried. This thing is bigger than just us now." He turned on the ignition. "I think we need to talk to Lucy and Richard and Gran and tell them everything we know."

"And Mark," she said.

"I think you should ask them what they want to do and then put an end to this."

Deena was surprised by her husband's suggestion. "You aren't thinking about taking the money, are you?"

"Absolutely not," Gary said more calmly. "Who knows, maybe the book will come out and be seen as just another failed attempt to complicate what was really a simple case—one lone nut pulling off the crime of the century."

"You're right. Maybe I should just call Donna and cancel the meeting."

He shook his head. "I know you. You will always wonder what she might have said. Besides," he added, "you wouldn't want Mrs. Fitzhugh to have covered her best dress in hot tea for nothing, now would you?"

Chapter 31

Full of nervous energy, Deena decided to clean out the refrigerator and pantry. Maybe she would take up cooking since she obviously was not cut out for investigative reporting. She was picking Russell up at seven o'clock. He insisted on getting the hotel room, telling Deena it would be a surprise. She already packed an overnight bag and put it in the car. The rain had slowed to a light drizzle, and she hoped it would stay that way.

Her refrigerator looked like a science project. Fruits, vegetables, and leftovers in various stages of decay seemed more like abstract art than consumable food. She pulled the trash can over and repeated the ritual she had performed on her car. Some of it was too disgusting to bother removing from the plastic containers. She threw them away, lids and all. A bag of lettuce had turned to liquid. Tomatoes looked like prunes. If it was wrapped in foil, out it went. This was just the fresh start she needed.

The pantry was not much better. She found four nearly empty bags of chips. Hidden behind the soup and jars of spaghetti sauce was a moldy bag of bread. Three half-empty boxes of cereal were pushed to the back. She checked the expiration dates. Two were almost a year old. These must have been from when Gary went on that diet. The musty odor was not just from the bread. She pulled out a bag of potatoes that had roots the length of her hand. *I can't grow roses, but potatoes I'm good at.* By the time she was finished, she had filled two large plastic bags. Good thing Gary wasn't coming home for dinner. She had totally lost her appetite.

Opening the blinds in the den filled the room with a wave of dust, little sparkles catching the few rays trying to peek from behind the clouds. Maybe I need a maid like Mrs. Fitzhugh, she laughed to herself. Preferably, someone who would also cook. She sat at her desk and decided to continue reading through the stack of Gran's correspondence. The first was a letter from a cousin in Missouri, dated 1939. The letter told about her husband's new job and the baby's illness (croup, of course) and the visit from another cousin—typical life for that era. She read several postcards from places around the country, all wishing the Meade's well and hoping to see them soon.

One stack of letters was bound with a brittle rubber band that broke apart when Deena tried to remove it. These were letters to Gran and Grandpa from Matthew when he was stationed overseas. An hour flew by as she read letter after letter, each with the same greeting: "Dear Mama and Papa, I am fine." He would go on to tell them some little story about what he had eaten or what he and some of his buddies did for fun. If she hadn't known these were wartime letters, she'd have thought he was away at summer camp. No details of the harsh conditions or brutal missions. All the letters were white washed as clean as Tom Sawyer's picket fence.

As she got up to add these to the box of pictures, another letter on the desk caught her eye. It was sealed shut, nothing written on the outside. She sat back down to read it.

Dear Mom and Dad,

If you are reading this, then you know that I am dead. I am sorry for the pain I have caused you by my actions. I took money to assassinate the president. I was blackmailed. I thought they would leave me alone, but they must have killed me.

Your loving son,

Matthew

At first, she was stunned. Then she remembered the joke Gary had made about looking for this kind of letter. Could he just be playing a trick on her? Purple roses, she noted, examining the border on the paper. It was the very same stationery Gran used for the thank-you note she sent.

Deena read it again, and then the truth hit her. Finally, something in this case made sense.

* * *

THE STOCKYARDS WERE hopping with live music despite the dark clouds and occasional brilliant flash across the night sky. Donna introduced her husband, and Deena introduced Russell. At first, Donna seemed suspicious, expecting Deena to be alone, but she decided Russell could stay. She told her husband to wait at the bar for her so she could talk outside on the patio in private. He handed her his jacket, saying she might need it if the skies opened up.

They sat at a metal table covered by a large Corona umbrella. Donna drank Bud Light and took long drags on a cigarette. She slapped at a mosquito on her baked, leathery shoulder where spaghetti straps revealed a lifetime of sunburns. Although her hair was over-bleached and frizzy, she still had a girlish look about her.

Knowing the clock was ticking because of the weather and Donna's time limit, Deena skipped the small talk and got right down to it. "First, let me ask you about the warehouse. Was there anything fishy going on?"

"You mean people stealing? Apparently so." Donna blew smoke out of the side of her mouth. It seemed to get stuck in the air around her face. "I didn't know anything about it until they were all fired. I think it was just a few of the guys involved, but I was clueless."

"Was that after Matthew disappeared?"

"Yes, about a week. I quit right after that."

"Didn't they fire you, too?"

"No. They knew I hadn't done anything." She took a swig of beer and glanced up at the clouds.

Donna had confirmed Gene's version of the story.

"What about Matthew?' Deena asked. "How did people feel about him?"

"He was really well liked. Very polite. A little shy, but very nice."

A waitress came by and Russell ordered a couple of beers.

Things were becoming clearer for Deena. "How did management find out about the problems in the warehouse? Did Matthew tell them?"

"Not that I know of. Honestly, I didn't pay much attention to what was going on at work. I did my job and that was it." She twirled a finger in the side of her hair. She might have been a dumb blond back in the day.

"Can you tell me what happened that last night at the café?"

"My car was in the shop, so Gene—Gene Collins— do you know him?"

"We did," Russell said solemnly.

"Anyway, Gene said he'd give me a ride home. Then he invited me to go to the diner for supper with him and Matthew, so I did. After we ate, I watched for my ride. He pulled up, I ran outside, and that was the last time I saw Matthew."

Deena felt her pulse quicken as she envisioned that fateful night. "What about Gene? Was he at the table when your ride showed up?"

"No. He had gone around the corner to the men's room, I guess. I remember saying bye to Matthew."

"Did you pay your check?"

"No," she said and chuckled. "I was in such a hurry I left my coat and forgot to pay my check."

It all matches up with what Gene had told them. "When was the last time you saw Gene Collins?"

"Let's see, it was the day they all got fired. Friday—I quit on Monday. Some people thought I got fired, but I didn't. I...decided to move back home with my folks. Never saw him after that. Is he in trouble for that robbery business? Is that what this is all about?"

"No," Deena assured her. "It's about Matthew. Do you remember a man named Glenn?"

"Glenn!" She looked like she'd just seen Elvis. "What do you know about him?"

"Just that you were seeing him at that time...and that he was married. Did he know Matthew?"

Donna looked back over her shoulder toward the bar just as the waiter brought the beers. "No. R.G.—that's what everyone called him—lived south of Bingham."

"Is that who picked you up from the café?"

"No, my brother picked me up. R.G. and I had gotten into a big fight. It was actually his fault that I was even at the café that night."

"What do you mean?" Deena took a sip of the beer Russell had given her. She would have preferred iced tea, but the humidity was dreadful and the drink was cold.

"You see, he came over on Monday night to see me. He had been drinking and wasn't treating me very proper, if you know what I mean. I told him he had better start being nice to me or I'd leave him for my other boyfriend. That's when he started laughing, saying I couldn't get another boyfriend if I tried."

The thunder crackled, but the sky held its water.

Donna continued. "Then I said, 'Not only do I have another boyfriend, but he knows all about you and me.' Well, that's when he lost his ever-lovin' mind. He started cussin' and fussin'. I should have known that would set him off since he had these big political plans, and our...um, *relationship* had to be kept a secret until he left his wife. I know now he was probably never going to do that. He wasn't jealous—he was worried about his reputation if word got out that he was cheating on his wife." She took a chug of beer.

Donna was getting worked up. Her ruddy skin reddened as she talked. "When he left, he went outside to the parking lot behind my apartment, pulled a tire iron out of his pickup, and went to pounding on my front fender. Luckily, a neighbor came out and scared him off. I had to get my car towed to the shop."

"Man, what a creep," Russell said.

"It gets worse than that," Donna continued, empowered by the booze and the nicotine and a sympathetic audience. "The next couple of days go by and he doesn't call me. Then late on Wednesday night after my brother dropped me off, he comes over after I was already in bed, smelling like a barrel of Jack Daniels, tracking mud all over my apartment. But this time he is being sweet and saying he's sorry." She took several more drags off her cigarette, and then dropped it on the ground, crushing it with her red stiletto.

"What did you do?" Russell loved a good melodrama. The humidity had turned to a mist, and he wanted to hear the rest of the story before the rain came.

"Dumb me, I decide to forgive him. That's when I tell him that I had lied to him before. I told I didn't really have another boyfriend. I just wanted to make him jealous, so I had made it up. I thought he'd be jumping for joy. But you know what he did? He threw up all over my living room floor. I couldn't believe it! He starts yelling, 'What have I done? What have I done?' over and over, stomping back and forth across the floor."

"What do you think he meant by that?" Deena asked, her stomach turning queasy.

"I don't know. All I know is that it went downhill from there. Of course, we were all worried about Matthew, but the following Saturday I came out of my apartment, and there was my car all fixed up. Inside was an envelope with four hundred dollars in it and a letter from R.G. saying that I was too good for him and that I should move back home. After seeing him act like a crazy man, that's exactly what I did. Good-bye, R. G."

Deena's brain crunched this new information. "So, on Wednesday night after you had dinner with Matthew, R.G. came to your apartment with muddy boots and smelling of alcohol?" She looked at Russell, wondering if he was on the same wave length.

"What were these 'big plans' he had?" Russell asked.

"I s'pose it doesn't matter all these years later. You see, he worked for the sheriff's department as a deputy. Hoped to be sheriff himself one day. Then governor. Only problem was that in small towns, they don't vote for men who cheat on their wives, at least not back then. That's why our affair had to be kept hush-hush."

A clap of thunder unleashed the rain that started pouring down in sheets. Everyone sitting outside jumped up and began running wildly, grabbing umbrellas, jackets, tablecloths—anything they could put over their heads as they ran for cover. Deena and Donna ran through the muddy slop and ducked under the patio awning. "My shoe!" Donna yelled.

Deena looked over and saw a red shoe stuck in the mud by their table. They watched people trying to pay their tabs, running to their cars, slushing in the mud. "I hope I answered all your questions because I'm getting out of here," Donna said as lightning and thunder cracked open the night sky.

The flash lit up a picture in Deena's head. It was Matthew. He was running through the rain with a coat over his head. "Donna, wait!" she yelled, trying to be heard over the racket.

"The raincoat you left that night at the café—what color was it?"

"Green," she yelled back and then disappeared inside the crowded bar.

"Deena, this way." Russell was standing in the parking lot holding the red and white umbrella, motioning for Deena to run to the car. She slushed her way over to the table and pulled out the muddy shoe. She wanted to take it back in to Donna. A loud boom of thunder changed her mind, and she ran to the car. She was soaking wet and out of breath. She threw the shoe on the floorboard by Russell's feet.

"The raincoat," Deena said, gasping for air. "Matthew wasn't wearing it when he was shot. He was holding it over his head to keep the rain off! R.G. probably threw it on the ground to cover Matthew's body."

Russell shivered. "Do you think R.G. shot Matthew?" He stared at his sister.

Deena turned on the car heater, not sure if the chill she felt came from the rain or the realization that the mystery was finally solved.

"Definitely, don't you? Why else would he have felt sick after hearing Donna didn't really have a boyfriend. He must have seen Donna through the window at the café and assumed Matthew was the man she was seeing. He worried Matthew might expose their affair and spoil all his political plans." Deena shivered. "I wonder if Carolyn Fitzhugh knew the whole story."

Russell shrugged. "It seems so obvious—except to Donna, that is. Why didn't you tell her? Why didn't you tell her she got an innocent man killed?"

"I couldn't, not after all these years. She didn't know that coward Glenn would assume Matthew was her boyfriend and kill him. It wasn't her fault. Like you said, sometimes the truth hurts more than it helps."

"I suppose you're right. After all, R.G. cared more about his career than he did her. Why make her suffer." He looked down at the muddy red shoe on the floorboard. "What are you going to do with Cinderella's slipper?"

"I don't know." She looked out the window. Cars were backed up, all trying to pull out of the parking lot at once.

"So, do you know R.G.'s full name?" Russell asked.

"No, but he's Carolyn Fitzhugh's brother. She called him Glenn." She looked in the mirror to see if the cars behind her were moving.

"R.G. Fitzhugh." Russell turned the name over in his head. "No, that's wrong. Fitzhugh is Carolyn's married name. Her brother's last name would be different, right?"

"Right." Deena repeated the name several times in her head. Without warning, she gasped and flung open the car door. She jumped out and ran to the back hatch to get something out of her satchel.

"What the heck?" Russell called out.

"R.G.," she said, getting back in the car. "The deputy who worked the Jane Doe case was named R.G." She looked through her notes and found where she had written it down during her meeting with Trey Simms. "Here it is. R.G. Brice. It all adds up now. Donna said he lived near Bingham and was a county deputy. When the remains were found five months later, R.G.—Glenn— worked the case and made sure Matthew's body was tagged as a female to keep it from being identified.

And, it would have stayed that way if Trey Simms hadn't found his skeleton fifty years later."

"R.G. must have followed Matthew from the diner and gotten him to pull over somehow," Russell said.

"And since it was raining, Matthew probably grabbed Donna's coat and held it over his head. Obviously, that's how R.G. got muddy feet that night. He shot Matthew and dumped his body in that farmer's field." She put the notepad back in her satchel and set it on the back seat. "Carolyn said her brother started drinking heavily after he broke up with Donna and got fired. Sometime after that, he died in a car wreck."

"Because of guilt, would be my guess," Russell said. Thunder crackled again. "Let's get out of here before we wash away. I'll give you directions to the place I picked out."

Fifteen minutes later, they pulled up to a motel in Arlington. "Why this place?" Deena asked, not recognizing it.

"This used to be the Inn at Six Flags. It's where Marina Oswald was kept while the FBI questioned her after the assassination of Kennedy." He grinned sheepishly. "It seemed like a good idea *yesterday* when I made the reservation."

Deena couldn't help but giggle. "At least now we have a way to stop Leon Galt from publishing his lies about Matthew."

There were several cars ahead of them under the striped awning at the front entrance. They decided to wait in line instead of dodging the rain to check in.

"What a night," Russell said, closing his eyes and leaning his head back against the headrest.

Thump, thump, thump. They both jumped at the noise against Deena's window. They looked out the foggy, wet glass to see Leon Galt standing in the pouring rain under a black umbrella.

"Geez, not him again," Russell moaned. "This guy's like Santa Claus. He sees you when you're sleeping. He knows when you're awake. Deena, what are you doing?"

"We can't just leave him standing out there," she said, rolling down her window. She motioned to Galt. "Get in."

Galt closed his umbrella and ducked into the back seat behind Deena. After a long pause, he said, "You found something, didn't you?"

His breath reeked of alcohol.

"How did you know we were here?" Russell asked, turning around in his seat.

"I called your house," he said and laid his wet umbrella across his lap. "Your friend Cliff told me where you were. It wasn't hard to convince him to give me the location once I told him who I was." Russell rolled his eyes. "Remind me to have a talk with Cliff."

"As a matter of fact, we did find something," Deena said. "We found out the real story about who killed Matthew. There was no conspiracy. No intrigue. Just plain old murder."

Galt waited for more information. "Is that it? Aren't you going to tell me the details?"

"Shoe's on the other foot now." Deena looked in the rearview mirror at his reaction. He was shaking his head in disbelief.

"I guess I can talk to Donna Morrison myself."

"She won't talk to you. I know you charmed Cliff, but she's pretty tough. Especially after I call her and tell her—"

"But can you prove it?" His tone had gone from curious to desperate.

Turning around in her seat, Deena began to feel sorry for him. After all, he had spent a long time on his research and was seeing it fall apart.

"Leon, this is a circumstantial case. Just as you said, we weren't there. But, when you put all the facts together, it is crystal clear what happened that night. I'm going to the sheriff's office tomorrow to give a statement, and then it will all be on the record." She was tempted to add, *You can be one of the first to read it.*

Galt lowered his head. "I had a hunch this would happen. Just too many cracks in the tent poles. I know you won't tell me much right now, but are you sure he was killed that same night he disappeared?"

"Yes, because of the raincoat."

"The raincoat?"

"Yes. Donna left her raincoat in the diner and it was found with Matthew's body. It wouldn't have been there if he had been killed a month later."

"No. You're right." He stared down at his hands, gripping his soggy umbrella.

Russell motioned for Deena to move the car forward as one of the other cars in front of them pulled away. "I'm going to check us in." He looked back at Galt and said, "Don't do anything stupid." He got out of the car and sprinted to the door.

"It wasn't just a book deal," Galt said softly. "They were talking feature film. A documentary. The whole nine yards.

This could have been the big payday I have been working for all these years."

Deena thought he might be about to cry and turned back to face the front of the car. "The thing is, Leon, your story isn't true—not this part anyway. Doesn't the truth mean anything to you?"

Deena waited for him to speak. The awkward silence was deafening. But then she felt something press against the back of her neck. It was cold metal. She froze.

Galt spoke slowly, taunting Deena. "Have you ever thought about that night? How must it feel to have a gun pointed at the back of your head, knowing—not wondering—but *knowing* it is about to go off? Do you think he was pleading for his life or praying for his afterlife?"

Sitting perfectly still, Deena held her breath. Shifting her eyes to the mirror, she saw the neon light from the motel sign flicker off the steel barrel. Now she wished Russell had left the gun in her glove compartment. He's not going to shoot me, she thought. Surely, he's not that drunk.

"Leon," she said.

"Shut up, I'm thinking." In the mirror, she watched him reach up and touch the bandage that covered the stitches on his forehead.

Deena knew he only had one good hand. She felt him push a little harder against her neck. Where was Russell? What would Lara Croft do?

"Let's go," he said. "Drive."

That was the last thing she wanted, so she started to move toward the car door.

"Drive!" He pushed the metal shaft into her neck and then up on her head.

She put the car in gear and maneuvered around the sedan that was stopped in front of her. She glanced to the right. No sign of Russell.

The motel was on the highway and there was only one road to take out of the parking lot. She pulled out onto the access road.

"Get on the highway," he ordered, his voice more sinister than before.

Deena did as instructed. Her cell phone rang. Probably Russell. He would call the cops and tell them the description of her car. However, she knew this stretch of road was a notorious speed trap. If only she could find a cop and get his attention. She started to weave a little onto the shoulder. *Come on, Mr. Policeman. Reckless driver here.*

"Stop that!" The shout from the back seat startled her, and she jerked the wheel to the right toward the shoulder. When she did, Galt fell to the side, catching himself with his right arm. That's when she saw it. In his hand was not a gun or pistol or revolver—whatever they call it—it was his umbrella. She had just been carjacked by a sleazy, greedy, umbrella-wielding hack from New York City! She pulled to the side of the road and stopped.

Knowing he'd been found out, Galt opened the door, got out, and started walking back from the way they came. He struggled to open his umbrella that had smashed against the car seat.

"Just wait!" Deena shouted, getting out of the car. "I'll have you arrested! You'll be in jail! Can't wait to read about it in your next book!" She blinked her eyes to see through the rain soaking her face. She reached into the car and pulled out the muddy stiletto. Rearing back, she threw it as hard as she could, nailing her target in the back of the head. He fell to his knees, wobbled, and then just fell back on the ground defeated.

She sat in the car with the door open, one leg hanging outside, ready to pounce on her prey at a moment's notice. She dialed 9-1-1 and then called Russell. Barely a minute later, she heard a siren. The highway patrol car pulled in front of her and two officers jumped out. They walked toward Galt—guns pointed—who was holding the back of his head with his one good hand.

"Nice shot," he said as they approached.

"Stay right there!" one officer ordered.

"Don't ever underestimate a country girl!" Deena shouted.

The other officer put his hand out to keep her back. "I need you to come to the station to make a statement, ma'am."

She watched as they handcuffed Galt and put him in the squad car. Another police car pulled up. Russell jumped out of the back seat and ran to his sister.

"What did that guy do to you?" he asked, looking her over for signs of trauma.

"I'm fine. I'll tell you all about it at the station." Tears started running down her face, mixing with the rain, as she thought about how lucky she was to have Russell in her life. They trotted back to her car.

One of the officers came up and gave her directions. She waited as both cars pulled away.

She turned to look at her brother. "I can't believe you got that psycho man's autograph."

Russell grimaced. "At least I didn't bring him cookies."

Chapter 32

It was late by the time Deena and Russell got back to the hotel. She spent another hour explaining to Gary over the phone everything that had happened. With her head aching and her nose running, she plopped down on the bed and fell fast asleep. Her cell phone rang at seven-thirty the next morning. It was Aunt Lucy.

"I'm sorry to call so early, but Mama had another terrible fright last night. She says she had another visit from Matthew's spirit. Is there any chance you could come here and give her reassurance? She seemed much better last time after your visit."

"As a matter of fact, I was planning to come this afternoon. I think I finally have answers for her, answers that should let her rest in peace. Wait—bad choice of words."

"I know what you mean, dear."

Deena explained that Gary and Russell would be coming and asked her to make sure Mark would be there, too.

Deena's breakfast consisted of coffee with a side of more coffee. Russell was starving. She told him she wanted to talk to Trey Simms at the sheriff's office before going to see Gran.

Russell smeared grape jelly on an English muffin, waiting for his coffee to cool. "Are you going to tell him everything we found out?"

"Since the murderer is one of their former deputies, I think they should know. All the evidence is circumstantial, but maybe they can at least close the case. Also, if Galt ever tries to stir up trouble again, the information will be on the record." Deena wiped at the drops of coffee she spilled on her blouse. "This was odd," she continued. "When I talked to Deputy Simms this morning, he said he has something he needs to tell me about Matthew's case. I wonder if he got another tip."

Russell stabbed his hash browns with his fork. "Maybe Leon Galt showed up and confessed."

"I HOPE THIS IS THE last time I have to come here for a while," Deena said as they got out of the car. They went to the front desk and Deputy Simms came out to escort them to his office. She introduced Russell.

"I'm glad you called," Simms said. "I know you found some new information, but there is something I want to tell you first."

"Fire away," she said and glanced at Russell.

"It's about R.G. Brice. He investigated the Jane Doe case."

"I know," Deena said. "You gave me his name when we first talked."

"I should have told you this before." Trey squirmed a bit in his chair and began tapping his pencil on his desk. "You see, R.G. Brice was my grandfather."

"What?" Had she really heard him correctly?

"He was my grandfather, Roy Glenn Brice, Sr."

"But your last name—"

"I know. In late 1964, my grandfather was no longer working for the department. He died not long after that in a car accident. My grandmother remarried and her husband adopted my father, R.G., Jr. When I came along, my parents decided to keep the tradition alive."

Deena looked down at the engraved nameplate on his desk. "So, you are R.G. Simms, III—Trey."

"That's right. I was too embarrassed to tell you before, seeing how my grandfather had done such a lousy job investigating the Jane Doe case. It was probably his fault Matthew Meade was misidentified as a female."

Russell's face had turned the color of melting snow. "Are you related to Carolyn Fitzhugh?"

"She's my great aunt. Do you know her?"

"We've met." Deena clutched the satchel in her lap, unsure of what to do. Should she tell Trey his grandfather was a cheat and a murderer?

Trey looked at Deena then Russell, both still as statues. "So, now that I got that off my chest, what new evidence do you have about the case?"

"Um, uh, about your grandfather," Deena said. "I mean, about the case. I suspected something was unusual when I first talked to you, but this explains it."

"You must be a pretty good investigator to have picked up on those clues. What about that lead I gave you? Did you talk to Henry Wilcox?"

"Turned out to be nothing," she said. "Just a disgruntled former employee looking for some attention."

"We get a lot of that kind around here, I'm afraid."

"I was able to find Donna Morrison." Deena fidgeted with her satchel to buy time while she was thinking. She needed to tell him something. She could feel Russell's stare as she pulled out a legal pad and flipped through the pages. "Yes, here it is. The green raincoat. The one found on Matthew. It turns out it was Donna Morrison's."

"I see," he said, and scribbled on a notepad.

"He wasn't wearing it but was probably using it to cover his head. Whoever shot him probably threw it on top of his body."

Trey nodded. "I'll make a note of that."

She proceeded to tell him about her run-in with Leon Galt. The deputy became more serious and assured her he would follow up on it.

Deena glanced at Russell and stood to leave. "Thanks for your honesty, Trey. It's been nice working with you."

"Remember, if anything turns up, the Bingham County Sheriff's Office is always here to help."

They left the office and got back in the car.

"Don't say it," she warned Russell.

"I can't believe Trey's grandfather murdered our cousin, and we are the only ones who know."

Deena covered her heart with her hand. "I didn't know what to say. What would you have done if you were me?"

Russell sighed. "Probably the same thing."

"Let's get back to Aunt Lucy's house. I have a bone to pick with Mark."

Chapter 33

The summer storm's cleansing bath had brought about a renewed spirit. Dust turned to mud then washed off the roads and trees. Even the weeds looked better. Lucy's yellow and pink roses were full and happy after a thirst-quenching drink of water. Deena hoped she could raise the spirits of the family just as much.

Inside the house, Mark paced back and forth like a nervous tiger. Gary sat on the sofa drinking a cup of coffee. Gran was dozing in the rocker. Uncle Richard and Aunt Lucy worked crossword puzzles at the kitchen table. When Deena and Russell walked in, everyone seemed to relax—everyone except Mark. Richard brought in kitchen chairs for extra seating.

"Did Matthew shoot the president?" Gran asked in a groggy voice.

Deena's heart skipped a beat. "No, of course not! Who said anything about that?" Maybe Gran knew more than she had said.

"I may be old and frail, but I am not deaf." She pointed at Mark. "I heard you talking on the phone to someone about it. That's what you think, don't you?"

Everyone looked at Mark.

Russell was particularly annoyed with his cousin. "Why would you say that without having all the facts? We know you were working for Leon Galt, but this is taking it too far."

"Leon Galt? That man from New York?" Richard asked.

Mark's face reddened under the scrutiny. "Noel Future is his penname. He has evidence about Matthew's involvement in the assassination. Ask Deena, she'll tell you the same thing."

Deena leaned forward on the sofa. "Did you know Leon Galt tried to kill me last night?" She heard several gasps. "Well, not really. He had an umbrella, not a gun. But he did carjack me."

Russell interrupted her. "It's a story for another time. Bottom line is, he was thrown in jail last night and showed his true colors. It was all about the money for him."

"Also," Deena added, "he told Gary and me what he thought, and believe me, he had no hard proof of Matthew's involvement. Only speculation."

Mark stopped pacing long enough to return her stare, but then looked down without answering. Richard stood up and pointed to a chair. "Sit down, son, and talk to us."

"Did Galt pay you to follow Deena?" Russell asked Mark.

"He gave me some money."

Lucy gasped and shrank back against her husband, covering her mouth with both hands.

Mark seemed unmoved. "It wasn't nearly the amount he offered Deena and Gary. I would have gotten more if she had just gotten Gran to sign the form."

"Sign a form?" Gran repeated softly. "Oh dear," she said and her face turned ashen. "That's what Matthew's ghost asked me to do last night. It was so real. He took my hand and tried to put a pen in it. That's when I hollered."

Deena reached over and squeezed her hand. "It was no ghost, trust me. Would you care to explain, Mark? And start with the letter you left when you were at my house."

"Mark! What have you done? Tell us," Richard demanded.

"This is ridiculous," Mark said. "I'm leaving."

"Oh no you're not," Gran said, and reached out with her cane, catching Mark's foot. He tumbled into the middle of the room landing face first on the rug.

"Touché!" Deena yelled, a little too loudly.

Russell helped him up and took him back to his chair. "Why don't you just relax and tell us all about it."

"Why don't *you* tell them since you seem to have all the answers." Mark rubbed his elbow and glared at Deena.

"My guess is Galt offered you money to follow me, but you decided to add some extra services on your own. You went in to Gran's room one night when she was asleep and got a piece of stationery out of her night table. That was your first ghostly visit." Deena pulled the note out of her bag. "Does this look familiar?"

Mark shrugged and looked away.

"It's a note supposedly from Matthew admitting his involvement in the assassination. It's fake, of course."

"How do you know Galt didn't tell me to write it?" Mark asked defensively.

"Because it was an amateur move. He wasn't trying to lie. He just wanted to get his book published. But you, on the other hand, had no problem with it. That's why you showed up at my house, to put this letter with the other documents I was going through. I'm guessing that you saw the thank-you note from Gran on my desk and got spooked, knowing it was the same stationery."

"Son, is this true?" Lucy asked.

"Yes. But I was only trying to speed up the process. I thought what Galt said was true—at least it sounded true."

Gran wagged her finger at her nephew. "How could you think your own cousin would have done something like that?"

He didn't answer, looking down at his feet. "I should have gotten different stationery, but I wanted it to look old."

"Good try," Deena said. "But it wasn't old enough. Remember, I know about vintage stuff. Something like that would have yellowed a great deal more. Maybe even have had paper mites. But that's not what gave it away." She read the opening of the letter aloud. "Dear Mom and Dad."

"That's not Matthew," Gran said. "He always called us Mama and Papa."

"I know. I read that in his letters to you." She looked at her grandmother. "He was a good son."

Gran's smile revealed the first sign of relief since Matthew's body was identified back in June. Deena turned to Mark. "So, you were the ghost that kept showing up at night. Shame on you for scaring an old woman like that."

Mark hung his head and mumbled something that might have been an apology.

"Richard, I want to change my will. I'm afraid your son won't be getting any of my money. It will all be going to Deena and Russell." She frowned at Mark. "It's not a fortune, but I bet it's more than you would have gotten from that New York shyster."

It was Mark's turn to pale and pall. He stood up again.

"Sit down," his mother ordered. "I want you to hear everything."

Deena sat staring into the distance, trying to come up with the right words. All eyes were on her now.

"Deena," Gary said gently.

She took a deep breath and turned toward Gran. "There was a woman who worked with Matthew. She had a very jealous boyfriend. The boyfriend was married, and he thought she was seeing Matthew behind his back. It wasn't true though. He was also afraid Matthew might tell someone that he was cheating on his wife." She covered Gran's hand with hers.

"It wasn't Katherine, was it?" Gran asked.

"No, this was after he called off his engagement to her," Deena said. "This man saw them together at the diner that night and probably followed Matthew and got him to pull over somehow, maybe pretending to have car trouble, flashing his lights...something. It was pouring rain, so Matthew took off his glasses and left his belongings in the car. He grabbed the raincoat the woman had left behind at the diner to cover his head and was probably forced into the man's car. The man drove him out to that remote field." She paused. "He covered his body with the raincoat."

"Do you know who that man is?" Richard asked.

"We have an idea, but he's been dead for years. From what we heard, he probably found out he had killed an innocent man and began drinking heavily. He died in a car wreck." Deena looked at Russell who nodded his head.

"So, he wasn't wearing the raincoat like the sheriff's office said?" Gran asked.

"No. It was probably just lying on his body."

Everyone sat quietly trying to make sense of the senseless act. Deena pulled the little address book out of her bag and handed it to Gran.

She clutched it to her chest. "So, my son didn't do anything wrong? He wasn't a criminal?"

"No. In fact, he was very well liked and respected." Deena took Gran's frail hand in hers. "It's still a tragedy, of course, but at least you have answers now."

"Bless you for all you have done. Richard, I want you to drive me to the cemetery tomorrow after I've had a chance to rest." She turned back to Deena. "I want to give you something."

Helping her grandmother up, they walked into the bedroom together.

Gran sat in the old rocker. "Open the chest for me, please."

Deena was surprised she was getting a rare look into the secret stash. She lifted the heavy lid and looked away, trying not to be too nosy.

"There's a box in the bottom left corner. See if you can find it."

Deena reached under the folded uniform and retrieved a cardboard box. "Is this it?"

"Yes. Open it."

She removed the lid and found a beautiful old camera inside. She looked up at Gran.

"Frank brought that camera back from Europe and gave it to Matthew. It was his most prized possession. We found it in the closet of his apartment after he disappeared. Now I want you to have it."

Deena was overcome with emotion. "I know this is a family treasure, and I will be sure to take care of it." She turned it over in her hands.

"I know you will, dear."

She recognized the Leica camera with a Zeiss lens as expensive and rare. Never having held one before, she admired it like a jeweler examining a fine diamond. She opened the film compartment and saw that it was empty except for a small scrap of paper. She read it and caught her breath. Then she slipped it in her pocket, hoping Gran didn't notice. After putting the camera back in the box, she closed the chest lid and stood up. "Do you want me to help you into the other room?"

Gran smiled sweetly. "No. I think I am just going to sit here and rest."

Deena hugged Gran and then walked back to join the others. Mark was still slunk down in the chair with his arms folded. She actually felt a little sorry for him.

"Don't worry about it, Mark," she said. "The important thing is that we now know the truth, and we can put this mystery to rest."

Chapter 34

Deena, Gary, and Russell agreed Las Abuela's would be the perfect place to celebrate, so the trio headed back to Maycroft. It was early, so they got a table in the bar and ordered margaritas, snacking on chips and salsa.

"Here's to a job well done." Gary raised his glass.

"Poor choice of words since I still don't actually *have* a job." Deena sipped her drink. "I can't really write a story and leave out all the juicy details. I guess this one will have to stay among us."

"Well, Labor Day is right around the corner—"

"Don't even say it," she warned her husband. "I'm done writing those articles."

He laughed. "I'll drink to that."

Russell glanced at the television over the bar as the announcers recapped the previous night's baseball games. "I'm glad they didn't ask for every little detail," he said. "That could have gotten tricky."

Deena nodded. "Sometimes less is more, I guess. Gran just seemed relieved to know Matthew wasn't murdered because of something bad he had done. I guess that was good enough for her."

"From the beginning, you said you wanted to help her get closure," Gary said. "You did that."

Deena looked at Russell. "I'm more worried about you, big brother. I don't want you to end up alone and cynical like Mark."

"That won't happen," he said with a grin. "I have Cliff and Maggie."

"Hey, I just thought of someone who is about your age and single." She winked at Gary. "Estelle Fitzhugh."

He turned to look at his sister. "Sounds as if Mark would like her. She's loaded."

Deena looked over to see Lloyd Pryor walk up to the bar and speak to the bartender. He turned around and saw her. "What are we celebrating?"

"Just the end of a very long summer," she said and introduced him to Gary and Russell.

"Rhonda told me you were investigating your cousin's death. What happened with that?"

"It's a long story," she said, "and not one I can write for the newspaper."

"Well, I'm glad I ran into you. I was thinking about calling you in a few weeks. I need someone to cover the political beat, especially with local elections coming up. The sheriff's race in Bingham County is going to be a hot one."

Deena choked on a tortilla chip and reached for a glass of water.

"Really?" she managed to say.

"These kids on my staff think voter fraud has something to do with *American Idol*. One of the guys actually called Rick Bingham the President of Texas." The bartender returned with

Pryor's lunch order. "I need someone with some sense. Think about it and come by to see me next week."

Watching him leave the restaurant, Russell looked at Deena. "Did that really happen? Did you just get a job at the newspaper?"

"I think I did!" She smiled and shook her head in amazement.

"You see," Gary said, "good things happen to good people."

She leaned over and kissed her husband on the cheek. It had been a long journey, but she felt like she had learned some important lessons about life and about herself.

"Check out this play," Russell said to Gary. They both turned their attention to the sportscast.

Seeing that the boys were pre-occupied, Deena reached into her pocket for the slip of paper she had found in Matthew's camera. She read it again and then folded it up. Holding it over the red glass candle on the table, she watched the flames eat away one letter at time until its secret was fully devoured.

On the paper was written a single word: *Zoyenka*.

THE END

Want to continue reading the series? Check out *Sharpe Edge: Stranger on the Stairs*, book 2.

A HAPPY HOLIDAY OR A SILENT NIGHT?

A CHRISTMAS PARTY FOR the upper crust of the small Texas town of Maycroft turns tragic when the hostess ends up dead. Everyone assumes her death is an accident—everyone except her daughter, Estelle who turns to Deena to help solve the mystery. A jealous friend and a mysterious heir are just two of the likely suspects.

As a school teacher turned newspaper reporter, Deena must get crafty to dig out the truth before anyone else gets hurt, including her own brother, Russell. Not only is there a possible killer on the loose, but this may be Russell's last chance at true love.

Sharpe Edge is Book 2 in the Cozy Suburbs Mysteries. A little romance, some snarky suburban competition, and a lot of mystery will keep you turning pages in this clean, cozy whodunit.

Works by Lisa B. Thomas

COZY SUBURBS MYSTERIES
Sharpe Shooter: Skeleton in the Closet
Sharpe Edge: Stranger on the Stairs
Sharpe Mind: Hanging by a Thread
Sharpe Turn: Murder by the Book
Sharpe Point: Needle in a Haystack
Sharpe Cookie: Two Sides to Every Coin
Sharpe Note: Sour Grapes of Wrath
Sharpe Image: Danger in the Darkroom (Prequel Novella)

KILLER SHOTS MYSTERIES
Negative Exposure
Freeze Frame
Picture Imperfect

Acknowledgements

Thank you to everyone who encouraged me during the writing of this book. I had no idea it would be the start of a wonderful journey.

Thanks to beta readers, editors, friends, and readers. The support has been overwhelming.

Most of all, thanks to my husband who has always been a tremendous source of support and encouragement in everything I do. Without you, none of this would matter.